FATED
DESTINATION

D1598780

CARLA MULCAHY

I dedicate this book to:

My children, who have always believed in me, supported my ideas, and who have been my reasons to push myself to succeed. Kylie, Jamie, Amanda, and Brady, I love you!

My mother who has been my go-to person. Thank you for listening, loving, and believing in me. I love you!

My Aunt Debbie who has been a great friend and my wonderful cheering section. I appreciate all you do   for me! I love you!

And to all my family and grandchildren who make my life inspirational and blessed. I love you!

Table of Contents

CHAPTER ONE

OUR BEGINNING

The wind was blowing fiercely, and it was difficult for me to keep the car going straight down the road. My knuckles were white as I gripped tightly on the steering wheel and leaned as far up to the windshield as I could get to focus my eyes on the white lines of the highway as the rain poured down. I was relieved that my two little girls were sleeping soundly in their car seats, buckled in the backseat so that I could concentrate on getting us safely to the nearest motel.

Carrie was 3 1/2 years old and as bubbly as a child could be, with two little dimples on the corners of her mouth. Jenni was 11 months old and already extremely headstrong at her young age. She refused to take a bottle anymore when she saw that her big sister drank from a cup. She wanted one too. Both girls were young, innocent, and unaware of anything wrong or scary. I wanted to protect them and keep them unscathed of any harm or sadness in their lives; that was my job as their mother.

I married their father when I was just 22 years old, and he was 28. It didn't take long for me to fall in love with him. His charming, kind, sweet, and funny self won me over immediately. I worked as a cocktail waitress in a hotel Lounge called the Shanty Inn. The place was small and dimly lit, with candles on each table. The tables were elegant, with a smooth, shiny, black and white marble top. The carpet was dark gray, and the lighting was soft and dim, with two large chandeliers hanging from the ceiling. The bar top started at the entrance and curved around like a horseshoe. It had a glossy top that was also black and a small server opening at the end of the bar. I started working there when I was 18 years old when I moved out to California, and I loved working there because I felt like it was a classy place, yet the customers were friendly and down to earth.

There was a wedding in the next convention room the night I met my future husband. We were extremely busy and short-handed because the bus table person had called in sick, so I had to keep up with taking orders, serving the drinks and food, and cleaning off all the tables. I was exhausted by the night's end, and my feet hurt so bad that I was beginning to walk with a limp. I was at my last table checking to see if my customers needed one last drink before we closed when he suddenly appeared in the doorway in front of me. He shouted something to one of the guys at the table and began moving towards me.

"I'll take a Bacardi coke, sweetheart if that's no trouble." He said, smiling at me. I stood there and stared and blushed like a stupid little schoolgirl. I suddenly was stammering for words and had forgotten the drink orders I had just taken from the others at the table. I asked again for the drink orders, and a long-haired blonde, so pretty but with a bitch attitude, smarted off and said, "First day on the job, spaz?" I very calmly looked her in the eye. I smiled and, with very obvious sarcasm in my voice, said, "Yes, Maam, just out of the State Mental hospital today, have this here habit of chopping up Blonde looking Barbies with smart-ass attitudes." Everyone at the table burst into laughter except Barbie, who rolled her eyes in disgust.
I smiled proudly at my comment and hurried off to get their drinks.

When I set everyone's drinks in front of them, I collected the money from the gorgeous stranger and using both hands, he took my hand, placed a fifty-dollar bill in my hand, lingered a few seconds holding my hand, and said, "Keep the change sweetheart, and I would love your phone number." again, I was blushing, and I pulled my hand away quickly before he could feel my palms start to sweat. I smiled flirtatiously, said thank you, and walked away to go and put the money in the till. I could hear his friend teasing him about not getting a phone number from me, and I smiled as I eavesdropped on their conversation.

I finished all my cleaning while the customers finished their last drinks. Most of them walked out the door without being told, but there were a few left when Jimmy, the bouncer, hollered at them to drink up and told them it was time for them to go home.

Most of our customers listened when Jimmy said it was time to go because Jimmy was over 6 feet tall, had a big build and a beard, and had a gruff voice that made him look and sound mean and tough. Still, anyone who knew him knew that he was kind and had a heart of gold.

I washed up the glasses and went to stock the cooler in the back room, and when I returned, the place was empty except for the owner, Josh, and Jimmy sitting at the bar having a drink. "Hey, Kally, sit down and have a drink," Jimmy demanded. "Not tonight, guys; I am dog tired and am going home," I told them as I grabbed my purse and jacket. Josh got up from his stool to walk me to my car like he always did at the end of the night, and as I approached my car, I heard that familiar voice of the stranger that held my hand in the bar.

"Hey, sweetheart, I didn't get that phone number." He spoke. I spun around quickly to see him leaning up against the building. The lights in the parking lot were dimly lit and barely showed his form standing there, but I knew it was him. A chill went through my body, half nervous because I didn't know him and excited because I thought I would never see him again, but there he was.

"Hi again," I said, smiling. Josh stood close by me in a protective stance, and the stranger reached out his hand to him, "I'm Mike, and I am not a serial killer or a stocker," he said teasingly. Josh shook his hand and told him hello. Josh still stood by me, and I knew he wouldn't go in until I was safely in my car and on my way home, so I told Mike it was nice meeting him, but I had to get home. "That phone number? He winked at me, smiling. "Not tonight, maybe another time" I looked at him with a flirtatious grin, got in my car, and started the engine. Mike tapped on the window, and I pushed the button to open the window slightly. "When can I see you again? He asked. "You know where I work," I said with a smile. I waved to Josh and said goodbye, and I looked back at Mike, "Have a good night, Mike," I told him, putting my window back up. I backed up the car and sped off for home, leaving him standing in the parking lot with Josh.

When I got home that night, I crawled into bed exhausted but could not fall asleep, no matter how hard I tried. I kept thinking about this mysterious man that I had met. His hair was dark brown and slightly gelled to perfection, he had a small mustache that he trimmed neatly, and dark brown eyes, and when he looked at me, I felt like he could see right through my soul. I breathed in the smell of his cologne, which made me want to be closer to him. His hand was warm when he touched my hand, and I kept thinking about how my body trembled when he touched me. I knew I wanted to see him again but didn't think I would ever.

Finally, I fell asleep and woke up to the alarm clock ringing at 7 am. I sat up in bed and immediately thought of Mike again. I thought, "How silly; get up and shower, Kally, you idiot. You are never going to see him again". I tried not to think about it the rest of the day, but that night when I was getting ready for work, I took extra time in the bathroom putting on my makeup and getting dressed, hoping he might stop at the bar again. I wanted to look extra nice, just in case. I threw on a tightly fitted pair of jeans with a white blouse with big gold buttons down the front, leaving it open so that my maroon tank top underneath showed off just enough cleavage to be tasteful and sexy. I fixed my hair so my curls were hanging soft and loosely down my shoulders. I walked into work at 6 pm, and Josh looked at me, smiled, and pointed towards the bar.

I looked over and saw Mike sitting at the end of the bar near my workstation. He stood up as I walked over and reached out his hand. I went to shake his hand, but he placed one hand underneath my hand and put his other hand on the top, sending goose bumps down my arms and chills up the back of my neck. My heart raced, and I quickly pulled my hand away. "We meet again," I said. He smiled and said, "And we will again." I started to go behind the bar to clock in, and with my back turned to him, I said, "It's nice to see you again; I hope you have a good time tonight" I heard him say, "I already am sweetheart" I just smiled with my back still turned to him and pretended I didn't listen to him.

I only had to work until 10 pm that night, and he sat at the bar talking to Josh most of the night and a couple of other customers that sat down at the bar. I went about my business and did my job, and I caught him looking at me more than once, but then again, for me to catch him looking at me, I guess I was also looking at him, mainly to check and see if he was still there. He patiently waited all night until, finally, it was 10 pm, and Josh told me to go ahead and punch out on the time clock. I grabbed my purse and came back out front. Josh had already poured me a drink and set it next to Mike. "What is this?" I asked. "I never said I was having a drink," I told Josh. "Well, when a customer buys you a drink Kally, you should be sociable," he said teasingly and nodded his head at Mike. "Oh, I see; you two have already become buds and stick together, huh?" I teased back.

Mike patted the stool next to him and asked me if I would have a drink with him. I smiled at him, "Thank you," and sat down. "Can we go sit at a table?" he asked. I agreed, and we moved to a table in the corner of the lounge, away from the chandelier lighting, but the candle was flickering on the table, giving it a romantic atmosphere. Mike only had two drinks while waiting for me to get off work, which surprised me because he had been there for 4 hours. Still, I was glad that he was not intoxicated and that we could have a pleasant conversation.

Mike wore a nice pair of jeans and a black button-up shirt that slightly showed off his chest. He was extremely good-looking and very easygoing. He said he grew up in a small town in Oregon, Illinois. "My mom and my sister are the only ones left in Oregon. My father passed a couple of years back, and my sister moved back to Oregon to help my mom. She bought the house next door to Mom, and now she takes care of Mom's garden, mows her lawn, and helps her out with whatever she needs." He said.

"Do you go back and visit often?" I asked him. "I try to get home whenever I am on leave." He told me. My eyebrows raised questioningly, and he saw my puzzled look. "Oh, I'm sorry, I didn't tell you. I am in the Army and stationed here in Fort Irwin,". He spoke. "Oh, I guess I should have guessed that, with your short military haircut and the town being so close to an army base, huh?". I laughed.

He asked me my story, so I began," I moved to California a couple of years ago when I decided that turning 18 was my reason to escape my childhood and flee for a life. I just jumped in my car, packed full of clothes and family photos, and filled up with gas.

"When I was just 15 years old, I was in my room crying after one of many harsh encounters with my mother. I remember my dad coming into my room to cheer me up as he always did. My mother would tear me down, and my dad would try to build me back up." I continued.

"He pulled out this old map of the United States and told me to look at all the places I could go to follow my dreams. I hung the map on my wall and used to dream about escaping to one of those places one day. My daddy passed away a few months later from Cancer, and I always remembered his words," I told Mike with tears in my eyes.

"So, when I turned 18, I just closed my eyes, pointed to a place on the map, and headed for Newberry Springs full of excitement and enthusiasm. I rented a small house on the outer edge of town, and I immediately fell in love with the small-town population of just over 4,000. I landed a job at the Shanty Inn within a couple of days, and I found a house as soon as I drove into town." Mike was easy to talk to.

"The first place I saw had a big red "for rent" sign in the yard, and I pulled in. It was almost like it was my destiny to be there." I looked into Mike's eyes as he listened politely. "Well, I am glad you moved here, Kally," Mike said with a wink. He placed his hand on my hand, and I didn't pull it away this time.

Before we knew it, Josh was at our table telling us it was "Last call" at the bar, and neither of us wanted another drink. I told Mike that I better get home.

We got up from the table, and he walked me to my car. "Can I have that number yet?" He asked. I smiled and told him yes. I told him my number, and he wrote it down on a napkin, folded it neatly, and put it in his wallet. "I had a nice time, Kally" he smiled and reached for my hand. He pulled me closer to him and kissed my cheek. "I'll talk to you soon," he said and opened my car door for me. I said goodbye, got in my car, and drove home smiling three blocks to my house. Before I got to my front door, my cell phone was ringing. "Just wanted to make sure you got home okay." It was

Mike. Laughing, I said, "Yes, I just opened my door." "Thanks for a nice evening, Kally; sleep good, sweetheart," he said. Something in his voice when he talked just set my soul on fire. It made me desire him without even seeing him. "Goodnight Mike, I had a nice time as well," I said, smiling.

When I decided to move out to California, my mother gave me an ultimatum. She said, "Kally, if you decide to move out there, then you can consider me dead" I was devastated that a mother could say that to her daughter, but we had never been that close, and after my father had passed away, it became worse. My mother dished out the punishments in our family, and she could be cold as ice. My dad was a gentle but firm man, and he and I had a close relationship. He praised me for everything I accomplished, and even though I was a bit of a wild teenager at 15 years old, he had faith that I was only going through a phase and would eventually find my way.

My Mother and I often butted heads, and I knew I would be miserable if I stayed. So, I took my mother's ultimatum with a grain of salt and chose to leave. I tried several times to call and talk to my mom, but she always had a way of cutting everything I did down, so eventually, I quit calling and found my way on my own.

I only had one brother that was older than me by five years, and he moved away as soon as he turned 18. He didn't get along with my mom either, so as soon as he could escape, he was gone. He used to call once and a while, but that faded too, and to this day, I have no clue where he is.

I guess some families are close and stay connected throughout their whole lives, but that was never my family. My mother chose to be alone, and I seriously don't think she has any regrets. She told us that if it were up to her, she would have never had any children, but Daddy wanted kids, and I guess she gave in to him on that subject. I always swore that if I could find a loving man like my father, I would hold him close, be kind and caring, and have a boatload of kids with him to fill our happy home. I also swore that I would make a great mother, so I guess Mamma taught me how NOT to be. I will give her credit for that.

The next day I couldn't get Mike off my mind, and I was anxious for the next time he would call. I had his phone number saved in my cell phone now, but I wanted him to be the one to contact me. I was sure he probably was currently working, and I didn't want to bother him. That night he called, and we talked for over an hour. I wasn't working that night, but he couldn't come off base due to some training exercise he had to do bright and early in the morning, but he told me that he was going to be on leave for the next two weeks and asked if I could get some time off from work and go with him to see his family.

"We could spend some time together and get to know each other better, and I would love it if you would join me." He said enthusiastically. I couldn't just go on vacation with him; after all, I had just met him.

That would be crazy, but part of me already trusted him so much that I wanted to spend more time with him. "Let me think about it for a while" He was satisfied with my answer and said goodnight. "Sweet dreams, Kally. I'll see you soon," he told me. I smiled and said goodnight.

Early the following day, I went to work and helped Josh clean up the bar and talked his ear off about Mike and how he asked me to take a trip with him. He told me it was too soon and tried to talk me out of it altogether.

"What's the rush Kally? Get to know the guy better before you leave the state with him. He could be a serial killer for all you know". He looked serious and playfully smacked my arm when I started laughing at him. I called Mike later that night, got his voicemail, and told him that the trip was too soon and that I didn't think it was a good idea until we got to know each other better. When two days went by, and I didn't hear from him, I began to wonder if he was upset with me about my message and would never call me again, but then the phone rang.

"Hey beautiful," his sweet voice rang through. "Hi," I said, trying not to show the excitement in my voice. I didn't want him to think I was sitting by the phone waiting for him to call me, even if it was true. "Sorry I couldn't get back to you sooner, we were in the field on a training exercise the last couple of days, and no phones worked out so far in the desert," he explained. "It's okay; I have been busy anyway," I lied. "Well, my vacation starts in about 10 minutes, and I would love to take you out to lunch if you aren't too busy?" he teased. "That would be fine," I told him. He said, "See you soon then." I hung up the phone and ran to the bathroom, ripping off my clothes in a hurry to jump in the shower and clean myself up.

I was a mess from cleaning all morning at the bar and smelled of bleach. I was finishing up my makeup when I heard his car pull up out front. I quickly grabbed a pair of sandals to match my white shorts and a pink tunic tank top that showed off my tanned skin. I took one more look in the mirror and decided I looked pretty good, smiled at myself, and went to get the door. I opened it, and he immediately grabbed me up in his arms and kissed me passionately before I could catch my breath.

My body was in his grasp, and there was nothing I could or wanted to do to stop it. When he finally let go and stepped back, he was smiling and staring at me, and I felt like I needed to sit down before falling. "I missed you like crazy, Kally; I hope you didn't mind," he asked. "Is that all you got?" I teased. He grabbed me up again, and I was ready for it this time.

I kissed him back with everything I felt in my body, and his hands gently slid down my back until they reached the small of my back, and he pressed me closer to him. He moved down to my neck and tilted me backward, still holding me close. My knees grew weak, and I couldn't hold myself up. We sank right there in the middle of my dining room floor and his body on top of me, gently holding himself up but close to me still.

He kissed my neck and then moved down my body as he slid my straps off my shoulders. I could feel myself trembling in excitement, and I could swear he could hear my heart pounding. He suddenly rolled over, pulled me on top of him, put one hand on the back of my neck, and pulled me down. I kissed his soft, warm lips like I never wanted to stop. My body wouldn't let me stop, I wanted this to last forever, and for that moment, I utterly lost myself in another world.

I was not a virgin. I had been with a couple of other men that I thought were the love of my life, but I had never felt like this before, and I did not want it to end. We made love as we had never made love to anyone before, and afterward, we lay there on the floor like we both couldn't move. He held me close to his chest, and I could hear how fast his heart was racing, just like mine was. We connected as if we had known each other for years.

We did not go to lunch that day. In fact, we made it as far as the bedroom, where we stayed until morning—making love, resting, making love again and again. I fell asleep in his arms and awoke to the sun peeking in the window.

I rolled over to look at my alarm clock and saw that it was 6 am, and my stomach was growling with hunger. I quietly put my feet on the floor and reached for my robe, trying not to disturb Mike as he lay sleeping in my bed. I crept out to the kitchen, started the coffee pot brewing, and then went to get in the shower.

Mike woke up at 8:30 am, and I was dressed, with makeup on, sitting at the kitchen table reading the newspaper and drinking coffee, when he snuck up behind me and kissed me on the neck, sending a shiver down my spine. "Good morning, sweetheart," he said, smiling with his beautiful brown eyes looking at me. "Morning," I said and returned a smile. "By the way, last night was amazing," he whispered in my ear and brushed his cheek against mine. I blushed and got up to pour him a cup of coffee.

We sat down together, and again; he asked me to come with him to meet his family. "Mike, I just can't run off to another state with you after only knowing you for a few days.

That is simply crazy!" I shrieked. "Take a chance, Kally and I just know we will have the time of our lives together," he told me. We ate some eggs and toast for breakfast and cleaned the kitchen together. "I'm going to go pack a few things, and I will be back to pick you up at 4 pm if that will work for you?" he said with a sexy smile on his face waiting for me to say yes. I shook my head no, and he took my hand and pulled me to him, "Come with me, Kal, two weeks together! It will be amazing, honey," he begged.

"Let's do it," I shrieked, and he grabbed me up and twirled me around in excitement. He went home to pack, and I called Josh to let him know. "My God, Kally, are you nuts?" Josh was upset, and I knew he would be, but I just told him not to worry and that I would call and let him know how I was, and I would be just fine. I told him I had a feeling about this trip and that it would be amazing.

We hung up the phone, and I could tell he still wasn't very pleased and didn't exactly give his blessing to me, but he knew he wasn't changing my mind either, so he gave up and told me to have fun. When I started working at the Shanty, Josh and I hit it off immediately. He became like a big brother to me, and sometimes he overstepped, but I knew he always meant well. He told me that I reminded him of his little sister. Since she lived on the other side of the country and he didn't get to see her very often, he was going to make it his goal to ensure I was okay.

After the bar closed and we were all done cleaning up, we would often sit down, talk, have a drink, and unwind before going home. He was at least ten years older than me. He began managing the bar/restaurant when he was 20 years old, and when the owners decided to sell, he quickly jumped on board and bought the business. I respected his knowledge in many aspects. I asked him how he got to be so bright, and he just shrugged and told me by reading and watching documentaries. He seemed to know many different things, so I often went to him for advice. It was great having him to talk to; he was hilarious too. He often teased and joked, and he always made me laugh.

CHAPTER TWO

OUR VACATION

Mike arrived at 4:00 pm, right on time, and I was packed and ready to go. I locked the door, and he reached for my hand and led me to his truck. Mike drove a White Chevy 1/2-ton pickup with a black stripe down the side. He opened the door, and I climbed up on the running board, with him gently nudging my backside to help me up in the seat. I buckled the seatbelt around me, and I immediately went to turn the radio on as I always do when I am in a vehicle. I turned it to a country station playing old-time classics, and Mike looked at me and rolled his eyes, teasing me. "Don't you like my music?" I asked. "I love your music," he said sarcastically. I just laughed.

We sped away from the curb and down the road to start our vacation together in Oregon, Illinois. I was excited to be with him but nervous about going so far away with a man I had just met not more than a week ago. Now I was going on vacation with him too. Everything was going so fast, yet it felt so right.

The first part of the trip was so long going through the desert and little to look at besides dirt and flat terrain, but we talked, and I sang to the music on the radio, and we both were so comfortable with each other. Mike reached over and held my hand and tried to pull me closer to him, so I scooted over on the seat until I was sitting next to him, and he put his arm around me then. When we went through Las Vegas, it was just getting dark out, and the scenery was much better. All the lights were fantastic, and I had never been there before, but I heard a lot about the city and saw pictures. The pictures could not describe the beauty and the glamor of the city.

We pulled into the parking lot of the Mirage, and we spent a couple of hours just walking around looking at the sights. Neither one of us was interested in gambling. Mike just wanted to show me some of the city.

At about 8:30 pm, we were back in the pickup, and I snuggled in close to Mike and fell asleep almost immediately. When I woke up, we pulled into a motel with a big red flashing sign that read, 'The Goodnite Inn.' I stretched and yawned and asked, "Where are we?" "Grand Junction, Colorado, you have been sleeping for almost 7 hours," he said. "Oh, I am so sorry; you must be exhausted," I said. "I am tired, so I thought we could sleep here for the rest of the night and then take off early in the morning," he explained.

"I am not tired anymore; if you want me to drive?" I asked. "I would rather lie in a bed with you in my arms for a few hours if that is okay?" he asked. I smiled and agreed that it would be nice. Mike went in to get the room key and then came out and drove the pickup around to the back of the motel nearest to the door we were staying in. He helped me grab the suitcases, and we carried them into the room. The room smelled of lilacs, and the bedspreads on the two queen size beds were gold and looked like they were from the '60s.

"Sorry, it's not the Ritz," he said, smiling sheepishly. "It's perfect," I told him, laughing. Mike pushed me teasingly, and I fell on the bed. "Ouch, the bed is concrete," I joked some more. Mike leaped towards me like he was going to jump on me but caught himself before landing just over me. I held my hands up to block him, laughing hysterically. Mike started tickling me then, and I couldn't stop laughing.

The room was absolutely hideous, but it was perfect because we were together, and he made me feel amazing. Mike fell asleep when I was in the bathroom brushing my teeth and putting on my nightshirt. I crawled into bed next to him, and he immediately rolled toward me and cuddled me close to him, still sleeping. I had plenty of sleep in the truck, so I thought it would be hard to get more sleep, but I fell asleep right away too. I must have been more tired than I thought.

I awoke to Mike kissing my neck, and my body immediately responded to his touch. I nuzzled closer, pressed my body closer to him, and we made love again. Soon we were dressed and ready to check out of the motel and finish our journey to Oregon, Illinois. We stayed overnight in a small hotel in Omaha, Nebraska, and went for dinner at a nice steakhouse. I had steak and shrimp, and he had broasted chicken. The meal came with delicious garlic dinner rolls, and the salad bar was terrific too. After dinner, we had a couple of drinks before returning to our hotel room.

We were both very full from our meal and exhausted, so after a quick shower, we both got ready for bed, turned on the television, lay in each other's arms, and fell asleep. 7 am the next morning, we quickly got ready for the day and completed our journey to Oregon, Illinois.

We pulled into the small town of Oregon at 1 pm. Mike said that his mom would probably have lunch ready for us, so we didn't stop on the way. I was getting hungry, so I hoped he was right. We drove by a historical little schoolhouse that someone took special care of preserving. I asked Mike about it, and he gave me a little history. I thought it was fascinating. He told me his great-grandmother went to school there when she was a child and that it had been moved and remodeled to preserve its beauty. It used to be out in the country, and ten children were in the class. They had walked from their farmhouses to the school, and there was a small playground outside. Mike said that if you drive down that country road, you could see a house built on the property, and they preserved the playground in their backyard. What a neat idea, I thought.

We pulled up in front of a mint green house with a white fence on the right-hand side of the yard. Many flowers surrounded the home, and a big picture window was right in front of the house. A deck was on the front of the house with a roof over the top and white pillars coming down. A swing was on the deck, and an old, frail woman was sitting on the swing.

"We are here!" Mike announced. I heard the woman loudly squeal when she saw us getting out of the pickup. "Mike honey, you're here!" she shrieked with delight. Mike ran up the three steps to the porch and wrapped his arms around her in a big hug. He then turned to me and held out his hand, "I want you to meet an excellent friend of mine, Mamma; this Is Kally," he said, smiling. I reached out to shake her hand, and she took my hand and held it tightly, smiling at me. "Nice to meet you, dear; Mike has been telling me about you." I smiled and told her it was nice meeting her as well. She looked more like she could be Mike's gramma than his mother, but I thought maybe she just had children later in her life. We went inside, and Mike was right; Alice had chicken sandwiches, grapes, and a salad waiting for us to dig in. We cleaned up after lunch and went outside on the porch to swing and visit.

We put our luggage in the bedroom where we were staying, and Alice gave me a quick tour of her home. Her house was cozy, neat, and full of unique trinkets everywhere. She had many figurines on shelves, family pictures hung up, and a gorgeous set of China in this beautiful oak cabinet in the dining room. I first thought of how difficult it would be to keep the house dusted with all these things, but I didn't see a speck of dust anywhere.

Mike told me that night after dinner that Alice was his gramma, and she raised him as her son all his life. He didn't discover that she was his grandmother until he was 16. Alice finally told him that his mother had run off when he was just eight months old, and she never heard from her again, so Alice raised Mike as her own. She was a wonderful mother to him and, now, was a wonderful gramma. He still called her Mamma, though, which I thought was sweet. "So, you don't know where your mother is?" I asked curiously. "No, and I haven't cared to look either," he told me. "Mamma told me she was a wild child that was out of control back then, and she was only 15 years old when she had me". He went on.

"Mamma tried to get her to settle down and be a mother when I was born, but she chose to run around with wild friends and drink too much, and she would come home drunk a lot. She was caught by Mamma shaking me when I wouldn't stop crying, and that is when Mamma told her she should leave and get her life together. Mamma told Evie that she could come back when she was ready to be a mother, but Evie never returned after that and never even called Mamma to let her know she was okay," Mike told me with his eyes blurring up. I reached for his hand and held it to my heart, "I am so sorry; that must be very hard on you and your grandmother." I told him. "I think it is more difficult for Mamma to accept. She seems so sad when she looks at Evie's pictures. That is Mamma's daughter's name." he said, refusing to acknowledge her as his mother.

I wrapped my arms around Mike and hugged him. He let me hold him in his arms for a brief moment but then let go and smiled, "let's go see if Mamma wants to play some cards," he blurted out, trying to change the subject quickly. I took the hint and followed him to the kitchen, where Alice was cleaning up the litter box of her kitten, Sally.

She was delighted to sit and play cards with us and then fixed us a light snack before retiring to her bedroom. Mike and I sat and watched television for a while until we were both yawning and ready to go to bed soon. The following day, we awoke to birds singing outside and the sun coming through the window. I could smell coffee brewing downstairs, and I grabbed for my robe that I had set next to the bed. I looked around the room and saw a sewing machine sitting on a table in the corner, and there were big, beautiful quilts that I knew Alice must have put together.

I admired the beauty and time she must have put into making these quilts, piece by piece. "Wow, your grandmother made these?" I asked Mike as he sat on the edge of the bed, pulling on his pants. "Yes, she enjoys making them and donating them to the church and the Good Will store in town," he told me. "Donating them? She could make a fortune selling these". I told him. "I know she could, but she gets more out of it by donating them to families that are less fortunate, she says" I nodded my head and smiled. We went downstairs, and I could hear Alice in the kitchen talking to someone. "Maggie's here!" Mike bolted down the rest of the stairs to the kitchen anxiously.

Mike had told me a little about Maggie, so I knew he called her his sister, but she was Alice's daughter, so that would make Maggie his aunt. At least, that is what I thought. I followed him to the kitchen, and he lunged toward this short, brown-haired woman. It was cut shorter in the back than in the front, and she had bangs that feathered to the side of her face. She was tall and slender with a beautiful smile and was very pretty. She was wearing a light blue blouse that showed off her white lace camisole underneath it and a pair of Khaki colored jeans that were straight-legged at the bottom showing off her white sandals and her brightly pink-painted toenails. She hugged Mike tightly, and he picked her up and twirled her around. When he set her down again, Maggie immediately came lurching towards me and hugged me, "You must be Kally," she squealed.

I uncomfortably hugged her back. "That's me," I said. "Mike told me on the phone that you were coming to visit our humble little town," she said as she stepped back to get a look at me.

"Wow, you are a beauty," she said in approval. I blushed a little and smiled. Mike took my hand and pulled me into him, "Isn't she?' he said. "Mike doesn't bring girls home, so you must be pretty special," she told me. I just smiled, still blushing, wanting them to change the subject. Alice must have felt my uncomfortable state because she blurted out, "Oh, stop all the babbling now and sit down for breakfast" I was relieved at that. She handed me a cup of coffee. "Thank you, Alice," I said. "You call me Ali, sweetheart; I hate Alice," she snarled, half smiling. "Oh, sorry, I didn't know," I told her. "It's okay dear; now you relax around us; we are family here." She demanded. I just smiled at her and nodded.

We had a wonderful visit with his family, and I admired how close they were and how Mike and Maggie had so much respect for Ali. I envied the love they felt for each other. I had not seen my family since I had moved to California, and I wasn't close to any of them since Daddy died years ago. We all had just gone our separate ways. It was lonely and sad at times. In the week that we were at Ali's home, I grew close to her, and she showed me her quilts and how she made them. She talked with so much enthusiasm in her voice, and I could tell she loved sewing and was good at it.

I was sad to say goodbye to both Maggie and Ali, but I hugged them and told them we would see them again soon. It was a great visit, and I looked forward to seeing Ali and Maggie again. I wondered how Evie could have ever left this loving family and if she

17

was also sad and lonely now that she had chosen a path without her family.

CHAPTER THREE

BACK TO VEGAS

Mike and I still had a week of vacation before we had to return. I thought we would stay in Oregon the whole time, but I found out later that he had other plans for us, and I was excited to spend an entire week with him alone. We drove straight to our destination, Las Vegas, NV, and I saw the beautiful lights again when we drove into the city.

This time we did gamble a little, and we went to a few entertaining shows, some magic, some dancing, and some singing. I had the time of my life. Mike kept looking at me and smiling. When I asked him why he told me that he had been to Las Vegas many times, but this time was the absolute best, just watching my face light up as I looked around at all the attractions. "It's like watching a kid in a candy store for the first time," he laughed. I playfully hit him on the arm and ran to the side to watch two ships coming out in the water and men and women dressed up as pirates, ready to dual one another. I watched with eyes opened wide and was fascinated by it all.

We had gone out to dinner one night, and just as we finished eating our entre, he reached for my hand and blurted out, "Marry me!" I sat there bewildered and amazed, not knowing if I heard the words correctly, and I stammered on my words when I finally cried, "What?"

"You heard me right, Kally; marry me! I love you and don't want to live one minute apart from you; you amaze me every time I look at you. My heart is no longer mine; you have it! So, marry me, please, and we will be as happy as we are right now forever; I promise you that." He said, and he knelt next to my chair, still holding my hand with one hand, and pulled out a ring with the other. It was beautiful. There are no words to describe its beauty. The Marquis diamond setting was in the middle of this silver band,

and two smaller diamonds on each side of it glistened in the candlelight.

I thought, oh my goodness, I have only known Mike for such a brief time, but it felt so incredibly right, so with tears in my eyes, I wrapped both arms around his neck, hugged him tightly, and whispered in his ear. "Yes, I love you and would love to be your wife."

"Let's get married here before we go home," he blurted out anxiously. With eyes wide, I agreed, and we were married in a small white chapel in Las Vegas the following night. We said our vows on June 7, 1986. I was the happiest I had ever been, and we celebrated our love that night in the hotel like it was the first time we had ever made love. I felt like nothing in my life could get any better. We stayed another night and celebrated and enjoyed the sights around Vegas. I was sad when it was time to go home, but I was going home as a different person. I was going home as Mrs. Mike Kalhoun.

When we got back to California, it was back to reality and back to work, and Josh couldn't believe his ears when I showed him my wedding ring. "You are crazy, Kally," he said as he hugged and congratulated me. Josh insisted that we have a small celebration, so the following Saturday, we had a DJ play some music at the Shanty. Mike invited a few of his buddies on base, and I asked the people I work with and a few close customers to join. I worked most of the time, so I didn't have too many close friends, well not any, to be honest. I spent time together with co-workers only. The Shanty was still open to the public, so we had quite a crowd that night, and Josh had hired a few people he knew to work that night so that the rest of us could relax and enjoy the evening. We danced and had a few drinks and celebrated as husband and wife. Everyone congratulated us and seemed genuinely happy for us.

Mike had moved off base and in with me, and we had moved a few things around in my house to accommodate his belongings and make it our home together. Ali and Maggie were ecstatic with the news when we told them after they had gotten over the fact that we did not have a big wedding with family and friends present, of course. Ali sent us one of her beautiful quilts for a wedding gift and a note that read,

"Welcome to our family Kally. I knew in my heart that you were the one for Mike as soon as I saw my babies' eyes shine the way they looked at you. I know the two of you will be very happy together. I am very proud to call you my daughter" All my love, Ali.

I was finally part of a family again, and I didn't think I could get any happier until I found out I was pregnant. I hadn't been feeling well for a couple of weeks. When I went to the doctor for a check-up to see if I had the flu or something, Doctor Jenson came in the room after running some tests and said, "Kally, you are going to be a mother." I jumped out of my chair, squealing like a hyena, and pounced at Doctor Jenson to hug him.

I left the office overjoyed, and after a couple of stops, I drove home to prepare for my evening when I would tell Mike. That night when Mike came home from work, I had made a romantic dinner for two, and on my way home from the doctor, I had stopped off at the thrift store and bought two bibs, one that read Daddy's Girl and one that read Daddy's Boy. Wrapped them both in a box with a note that read, *"Which one would you prefer, and what shall we name our baby?"*

Over dinner, I was chomping at the bit to give him his present. Still, I waited until after we finished eating, and Mike told me all about his exhausting day at work and how one of the tanker trucks had broken down. He spent most of the day fixing that. When he asked me how my day was, I took that opportunity and handed him his present.

"Well, I hope this makes your day a little brighter, honey," I said as I kissed him on the cheek and sat back down in my chair to wait patiently. "A present for me?" as he ripped open the paper and saw the note lying on top of pink and blue tissue paper, he read the message. He sifted through the tissue paper until he found the bibs. Before I knew it, he was on his feet and over to me on his knees in front of me, rubbing my belly, "Are you sure, honey? We are having a baby?" with tears in his eyes, he hugged me tightly and laughed at the same time. We both held each other and laughed and cried. I was so glad that he was as happy as I was.

The delivery was long and hard but worth the wait. Our daughter was born six months later, on December 15, 1986, and we named her Carrie Lee Kalhoun. She was 8 lbs. and 8 ounces and had a head full of black hair and the biggest, darkest eyes I had ever seen on a newborn. She looked like a little China doll as I held her in my arms for the first time. When they laid that beautiful creature on my stomach, all the labor pain went away in a second, and Mike was beaming with joy at my side. He looked at us both lying in bed and had tears in his eyes again. "I never thought that I could love another girl as much as I love you, Kally, but she takes a close second to you, my love" he kissed me gently on the forehead, and I knew that I must be the luckiest woman alive.

I motioned for Mike to take Carrie, and he picked her up, wrapped her in his arms, and sat down in the chair next to my bed. His eyes shined when he looked at her, and I could see what Ali was talking about when she said that Mike's eyes had a shine to them when he was in love.

I fell asleep, exhausted but extremely happy. I wished I knew where my brother was so I could tell him my news, but if he cared, he would have never abandoned me. I didn't bother calling my mother to tell her about my marriage or my new baby girl because I knew that her words would be ugly and mean. I was blessed to have Ali and Maggie as my new family; they were highly excited for us all.

At Carrie's second birthday party, I handed Mike another present. As he opened it and saw the same color of tissue paper with a note on top again, he looked at me with a bewildered, questioning look, "Is this what I think it is?" he asked, smiling. I nodded, and he was over to me in a second, twirling me around in his arms. Carrie didn't know what was going on, but she giggled at our silliness, and we looked at her and broke into laughter. She had chocolate cake all over her face and laughed with us.

Ali and Maggie had flown out to be with us for Carrie's birthday. They were all looking at us, wondering what was in the present that Mike had just opened and what we all were laughing about. "WE ARE HAVING A BABY!" Mike burst out loudly and full of excitement.

"Oh my, Oh, Oh," was all Ali could say as she held her hands up in the air in excitement and rushed over to me to kiss me and hug Mike and me. Maggie then followed and hugged us both too.

Our lives weren't perfect by all means, we had struggles with finances, household repairs, car repairs, and minor squabbles here and there, but it was perfect for us, and that was what mattered most.

When our little Jenni was born, it was 2 am, and after 12 hours of backbreaking labor, she finally made her presence in the world on July 7, 1989. The doctor held her up to me and placed her on my belly, and to my surprise, she looked a lot like Carrie did. Jenni had black hair and dark eyes and warmed our hearts immediately. She weighed 9 lbs. and 2 ounces and was absolutely beautiful.

"Another girl to love" Mike leaned down and kissed me. I was too exhausted to move, but I smiled as my eyes closed and slipped off to dreamland. When I awoke a couple of hours later, I saw my wonderful husband sitting in the chair next to me, holding our new little daughter in his arms, patiently waiting for me to wake up. "I'm sorry" I felt bad for falling asleep on him. "Oh, Kally, no need to be sorry, honey; you just went through tremendous work, baby; you have the right to rest." He leaned forward and took my hand.

"Can I hold her?" I asked, and Mike placed our little girl in my arms. I cradled her next to me and kissed her forehead as she slept. I stayed in the hospital for a couple of days and was anxious to get home. I missed Carrie so much. I was able to see Mike when he came to the hospital, but I hadn't seen Carrie in 2 days, and that was the first time I had been away from her.

When we drove up our driveway, Carrie came running out of the house with her gramma, Ali, right behind her. Ali had flown out to take care of me during my last couple weeks of pregnancy. She wanted to take care of Carrie while I was in the hospital. Carrie was so excited to see the new baby in my arms and was so glad that we were home that I thought she would knock me right over when she ran her arms right into my legs to hug me. I sank to her level and pulled back the blanket to show Carrie her new little sister.

Immediately, Carrie became as gentle as ever; she knew she had to be careful with this little dolly I had held in my arms. Carrie petted Jenni's cheek like a puppy and looked at her with amazement.

At first, I was afraid that Carrie would be a little rough and maybe somewhat jealous of the new baby, but that thought went away quickly when I saw that she knew right away that Jenni was a baby to be protected. Carrie coddled Jenni, gently petted her head, and kissed Jenni's forehead. That was her new little dolly, and she loved her.

Ali stayed with us for a couple more weeks to help me out, and I appreciated her kindness and was sad to see her go. Mike was in field training quite a bit and was gone a lot at that time, and I missed him so much, so Ali's help made it easier to be away from him. Ali also loved it out in California with us, she always had someone to play cards with and loved taking care of people too, but her heart was in Oregon, and I knew she would never leave her home there.

CHAPTER FOUR

FIRST TIME AWAY

Mike had come home from a week-long training exercise, and I ran to greet him at the door with Carrie on my heels. He hugged me as he was picking Carrie up at the same time. "Oh, I missed my girls," he said as he wrapped us both up in a bear hug and then, leaning in close to me, whispered, "especially you, baby, the things I am going to do to you tonight," he teased. "I can't wait" I gave him a sexy look and a quick flash of my shoulder and laughed.

After dinner, I bathed both girls and dressed them in pajamas. I went into the bathroom with Carrie to help her brush her teeth, and I could hear Mike singing to Jenni in the living room. I listened at the door while Carrie was busy brushing her teeth. "You are my sunshine, my only sunshine, you make Daddy happy in every way" he was making up his own words, and I listened at the door smiling with every beat of my heart.

Mike was such a good daddy; he showed us how much he loved us daily. He wasn't afraid to tell the world how he loved his family, too, like many guys I have met who talk about their wives as a burden when they get around their buddies.

Mike was not like that at all. He would come home and tell me that he does not understand how the guys could say such nasty things about their wives but still be married to them for years. I used to tell Mike that sometimes guys get together and need to talk like that to make them feel like men keeping up with their buddies. Mike would shake his head in confusion and tell me how dumb he thought it was. "If you are happy and in love, why not share that with them instead?" He would say.

After the kids were all tucked in their beds and asleep, Mike and I cuddled on the couch and watched the news on tv, and then I cleaned up the living room and started shutting the lights off. "Ready for bed, honey?" Mike said, stretching out his arms in a big yawn. "Very ready," I told him, rubbing my sleepy eyes. We retired to the bedroom, and I slipped on a nightgown, went into the bathroom to take my makeup off, and brushed my teeth. When I returned to the bed, Mike was lying on the bed, still dressed in his army uniform, fast asleep. I nudged him gently to try and wake him so he would get undressed.

Mike suddenly rolled over, opened his eyes slightly, smiled, and wrapped me in his arms. When he began to kiss me on my neck, he grabbed me and rolled me across the top of him onto the bed, and his body was on top of me, his hands sliding down my back to my thighs and pulling me close to him. We undressed each other with stimulating foreplay. My body responded as it always did when he touched me, and we made sweet love. It was beautiful how he could make my body react in a way I had no control. It didn't matter if I was exhausted; he always pulled me right into the mood with just one touch. Sometimes when I was doing the dishes, he would walk behind me, run his fingers through my hair, and when I would look at him, he would give me that flirty wink, and I instantly felt like dropping to the floor with him right that instant.

After we made love, he sat up in bed and told me that he needed to tell me something and that he was so sorry, but I wasn't going to like it. I sat right up, "Is everything okay?" I asked. Mike sighed loudly and touched my hand gently, "I am being called away on a training mission out in Maryland and have to teach a class for six weeks." He held up his finger to my lips to quiet me as I tried to protest. "Shhhh, it's going to be okay, baby; I will call every day, and it will go by fast; you will see." He told me. With tears in my eyes, I asked, "When do you have to go?" "I leave on Friday, baby," He said. I grabbed him and hugged him, and he held me rubbing my back, "It's going to be okay, honey," he kept saying.

I was used to Mike being gone out on field training close by, but he was always only gone for about a week, and then he was home again. That was hard enough, I thought. Six weeks is going to seem like forever. I kept thinking to myself until tears filled in my eyes. Mike held me tighter, tipped my face back, looked at me, wiped away my tears, and began kissing me again.

This time our lovemaking felt intense and fierce with passion, and there was a desperate urge to be as one that night. Tears streaming down my face, I let myself explore his whole body like a wild animal searching for its prey. Mike responded fiercely and kissed my tears away. He touched me in all the right places as he always did, but this time he took me like a fire inside of him was burning to be put out, and I surrendered myself to him in body and soul. I never knew love could feel this way, and I often wondered if everyone in love felt the same way that I did and if they did, why on earth did many of them seem so unhappy much of the time.

Friday came too soon, and I was helping Mike pack up the things he was taking for the trip when I just wanted to throw them all back in the drawers and closet where they belonged. Mike placed the last suitcase in the car and returned to say his goodbyes to the girls and me. He picked up Carrie and hugged her tightly and kissed her. "You be a good girl for mommy, and I will talk to you soon, my girl" he soothed her tearful face, and then he turned to Jenni and picked her up out of her playpen and held her high in the air as she giggled in delight.

I thought she had no clue how long he would be gone, but I did, and it was tearing me up inside. Mike put Jenni back down after kissing her and tickling her, and he reached for my hand as my eyes welled up with tears again. I fell into his arms and cried. "It's going to be okay, my love," he told me, brushing the hair that had fallen on my face. He kissed me on my forehead and took my cheeks in his hands, "I love you, baby! I love you so much, and I will be home soon". He kissed me passionately, and I heard Carrie giggling. We turned to her then and laughed at her big eyes, looking at us giggling, and we all began to laugh. I picked up Jenni and followed Mike to the car with Carrie beside us, and then we watched as Mike pulled out of the driveway and down the street.

He honked the horn three quick times and waved at us through his rearview mirror. We stood there waving, and my tears came again.

I quickly brushed the tears away as Carrie reached for my hand. "Daddy will be home after work, Mommy." She said with a smile. How will I explain to her when he doesn't come home tonight for supper? I thought. I just smiled at her and petted the top of her head.

"Daddy has to work for a long time, and he won't be home for supper tonight." I started with that, and she seemed to get sad eyes, but then she was off running to the house to watch her cartoons. I came in and marked the calendar on February 15, 1990, "Day left for training" I then carried Jenni over to the couch to sit and watch cartoons with Carrie, trying hard not to be sad in front of her.

Mike arrived safely in Maryland and called me several times on the way. I already missed him so much, and that night as I lay in bed, I felt just how much I missed having his arms around me with his hands touching my skin before drifting off to sleep. I disliked being in my bed all alone. I tossed and turned, and my sleep was interrupted. It is funny how one can grow accustomed to a new routine in such a short time. It never bothered me to sleep in my bed alone before I met Mike, but now it drove me crazy. During the day, the girls kept me busy. I took on a few more shifts at the bar while Josie, my babysitter, would come over to the house and watch the kids, but at night I crawled into my bed all alone, which was unbearable.

Mike called me every day as he promised, though, and I soon got used to him being gone, as much as I could anyway. My neighbor, Stacey, knew I was having a hard time. She tried to get me to go out with her on her ladies' night out, and I finally agreed one night, but I ended the evening by 10:30 pm. I rushed to the phone every time I heard it ring like it was the highlight of my days because it was.

"Come on, Kally, stay and have some fun," she protested, but I shook my head and made excuses of having a headache. I just wanted to get home and call Mike before I went to bed and before it was too late. Stacey and I were not all that close anyway, and she mainly talked with the other ladies, so it was a bit boring drinking by myself. I didn't consider myself a loner before I met Mike, but the friends that I did have were my co-workers at the bar. I worked as often as I could, and that was my socialization.

I only had one week left without my husband, so I painted the kitchen that week and changed the décor to kill some time. I finally decided on the colors to be a deep burgundy on one wall and cream on the other. I then bought a border to go around the top, which had the design of café, late, and mocha cups. I wanted to surprise Mike and make our lil' kitchen look like a comfortable little coffee house. I completed the project by Thursday, and Mike would be coming home by Saturday, March 3, 1990. I glanced around the kitchen, placed some potholders with the same décor by the stove, and hung a couple of hand towels to match. I was proud of my accomplishment and was sure Mike would love it.

I went to the market and picked up groceries to fill the kitchen so that when he arrived, we had plenty of food in the house and didn't have to leave for a while. Mike told me that after this training, he would be off work for a whole week to spend with his favorite girls in the world. I was so excited to see him, and I cleaned the house and kept myself as busy as possible so that the days would pass by quickly. That Thursday night, I went to bed and fell asleep immediately exhausted from all the work I had put into the house.

I awoke to a pounding noise and realized it was coming from the front door. I turned on the lamp and glanced at the clock on the end table to see that it was 2:30 am. I reached for my robe, threw it on, and went downstairs, turning on the dining room light as I came to the front door. I could see two men in military uniforms through my front door window, and my heart sank in fear immediately. I recognized one of the men, Paul Thorson; Mike had introduced me one night at the Military awards ceremony we had attended together.

My hand trembled as I opened the door, and they told me what I already knew. "Maam, I am sorry to tell you this, but your husband has been in a terrible accident and...." The voices drifted off, and my eyes saw white dots; my knees went weak.

I opened my eyes and thought I must have had a bad dream; I rubbed my eyes and opened them wider to see Paul sitting beside me as I lay on the couch. "What happened?" I sat up in a panic, pushing Paul back. "You fainted," he said softly. "Where is Mike" I screamed at him, crying then. "Kally, I am sorry. He never survived the ride to the hospital." I gasped for air, choking and sobbing, and I lunged at him and hit him and kept hitting him. I couldn't stop, and he just put his arms around me and held me tight as I pleaded with him to give me Mike back. Make this nightmare go away. This is not happening to us!

I screamed out in agony and pain. I thought it could not happen to us; we were so happy, and God wouldn't let things like this happen to such good and happy people. God wouldn't take away my girls' excellent., loving daddy and make them grow up without him.

I pleaded to God, "Give him back to me." Nothing I did brought him back. He was gone, and I was alone. Then the anger came, and I screamed at Mike. "You promised me you would be back soon," I cried. Paul sat with me as I sank to the floor, and he had tears in his eyes too. I am sure it was tough for him to tell me such terrible news, and seeing the pain he had brought to my doorstep must have been extremely difficult. I thank God that Paul stayed with me in those first few hours, or I don't know what I would have done. He sat on the floor and wrapped his arms around me, and rocked me until I fell asleep exhausted.

I awoke again, and Paul was still holding me in the same position, and I knew it wasn't a nightmare. Mike was gone, and I was alone, a single mother. "Oh God, how was I going to tell Carrie?" Jenni was so young that she wouldn't even have the chance to know what a wonderful daddy she had, and Carrie was so young that she would never even know him. "It is so unfair and so wrong," I thought to myself as the tears welled up in my eyes again. The mere thought of telling his Mamma, Ali, made me cringe. The news of Mike's death would crush her, and Maggie, too, would be devastated. They had such a close bond, and now Mike is gone from all our lives.

"Hello, Ali?" I said as I heard her voice on the phone. "What's wrong, Kally? You sound terrible." Her voice was filled with worry, as it should be, for I was about to send her world crashing down around her. "There's been a terrible accident...." I could not get the words out to tell her, and I burst into tears again and dropped the phone. Paul picked the phone up as I sank to the floor again, sobbing.

"Maam, this is Sergeant Paul Thorson. Mike was in an accident, and I am sorry, Maam, he didn't survive the crash" I could hear Ali scream out on the phone; it was the worst sound I have ever heard. I wish I were there beside her to hold her and tell her everything would be okay, but nothing was okay, and I knew that it would only be a lie I would have to tell her. Paul said he was sorry again and hung up the phone hearing no response but the sounds of Ali sobbing.

Carrie woke up crying, and I ran to her room to comfort her, and I held her so tightly, rocking her. "I had a bad dream, Mamma," she said with a scared, worried look. "Everything is okay, honey; Mamma is here with you" I soothed her and petted her hair away from her face.

"Why are you crying, Mamma," looking up at me, she noticed my tearful, puffy eyes and became worried. "I must have had the same dream," I told her. She seemed okay with that answer and told me it would be okay. I lay down beside her, and we fell asleep together. When I woke up again an hour later, I quietly slipped out of bed so I wouldn't wake up Carrie and Jenni. I went downstairs to find a note on the table from Paul telling me again how sorry he was and if I needed anything at all to call him. I was alone now to face my life without my dear, loving husband.

I made it through the day taking care of the children and putting them down for a nap around 3 pm. It was too quiet in the house, so I turned on the radio and tried cleaning up the toys the girls had taken out in the living room. The phone rang, and I let the answering machine pick it up, and when I heard Mike's voice on the machine, I dropped dead in my tracks. I ran to the phone and listened to my husband tell the caller, "You have reached the

Kalhoun family, but we are unable to take your call right now; please leave your name and number and we will get back to you as soon as we can, have a wonderful day" I played it again and again and again so that I could hear his voice.

The knock came at the door around 5 pm, and I was still listening to my husband's voice on the answering machine; I jumped at the sound of the knocking. It sounded loud and desperate. The girls were still asleep, and I quickly ran to answer the door so they wouldn't wake up from the pounding. Ali and Maggie rushed in to hug me, both crying. I stood there and let them hug me, but my mind and body didn't seem to feel anything. I was in a trance, and the next few minutes went by until I heard Ali say, "Kally honey, we are here for you. It is going to be okay" Ali was shaking me a bit to get me to snap out of my trance. "Nothing is going to be okay!" I finally snapped. "He is gone and never coming back, and nothing is okay about that, and it never will be okay!" I screamed out with anger. Ali just wrapped her arms around me and held me.

Ali took care of all the funeral arrangements, and I can barely remember attending the funeral. A co-worker of mine watched the girls during the funeral because I didn't think it was a place for them at such a young age. I guess I was there in body but not in mind. Maggie took care of the children after the funeral, and I slept a lot, unable to do anything productive without crying. It took everything inside of me to just put my feet on the floor, so I buried my head in my covers, trying to shut out the world.

CHAPTER FIVE

ENOUGH IS ENOUGH

Ali finally became frustrated with me, and she came to my room and pulled back the covers, "Get up, girl, this is enough! You have two babies that need you to go on with your life! They lost their daddy, and now they are losing their mother too. How dare you! Get up!" She screamed at me and opened the drapes to let the sunshine fill the room. I opened my eyes, saw her angered face with tears welling up, and I sat up to touch her hand.

"I miss him, Ali," I cried. Then, her face softened, and she sat down next to me. "We all miss him, honey, but you have two little girls that haven't seen much of their mother in three weeks, dear." She said firmly but softer. I thought to myself, three weeks had passed, and it felt like they told me my husband had died yesterday. I nodded my head and decided it was time to get up. I went to the shower and cleaned up, and went downstairs.

Carrie, wide-eyed, looked up at me, and a big smile came on her face. "Mamma!" She screamed and came running at me. I picked her up and hugged her. "Do you want pancakes for breakfast?" I asked. She nodded excitedly, patting her belly. I smiled at her innocent little face. I glanced around the room and saw Maggie on the couch holding Jenni, and I walked over, set Carrie down, picked up Jenni, and hugged her too. "Mamma, Daddy is watching over us in Heaven," Carrie said, looking up at me with sad eyes. I gasped a little catching my breath, and calmly replied, "Yes, baby, he is."

I gave Jenni back to Maggie and went to the kitchen to make pancakes. Ali had told the girls about their daddy. I was relieved that I didn't have to be the one that had to tell them, but I felt guilty that I wasn't the one to comfort their tears when they learned that their daddy wasn't coming home either.

Ali and Maggie had to go back home. For the next few weeks, I went to work, cleaned the house, took care of the kids, and did everything I was supposed to be doing. Still, it was like I was going through the motions but not enjoying anything anymore.

It was three months that Mike had been gone, and I began cleaning out a junk drawer one afternoon. I came across the old, crinkled map my daddy had given me years ago. I saw the big red circle I had marked on it when I pointed my finger and chose the little town in California. I opened it up, closed my eyes, spun it around on the coffee table, and pointed my finger to another place on the map. I opened my eyes to see that it had landed in Springfield, Wisconsin.

Everything here was just one big reminder of the life I had built with my beautiful husband, and I felt shattered and lost. Mike was gone for three months now, and I tried to move on, go to work, and raise the girls on my own, but it was too painful to stay here with so many memories of my beloved husband, so I decided that it was time to start fresh again and build another life somewhere else. I went to work the following day, gave Josh my two weeks' notice, and listened to his protest for over an hour until he finally hugged me and told me he understood why I was leaving.

I contacted a realtor in Wisconsin and told him I was looking for a small two-bedroom house in Springfield, Wisconsin, with a population of less than 3,000. I liked small towns and wanted to raise my girls in a small town with neighbors who knew everyone. I told my landlord I was moving, made plans, and started packing. I had some money saved up, plus, with the insurance money and Mike's death benefits, I figured I would be okay for a few months to get settled and find a job in our new place where we would make our home. I said our tearful goodbyes to our friends, loaded my girls in the car and started our new adventure.

Ali and Maggie begged me to move near them, but I needed a fresh start, and being near them would be too hard to get over Mike and move on. "I will visit you both soon, and I promise I will keep in touch; I just need some time," I told them on the phone.

On June 20, 1990, I left California and started the next journey as a single, widowed mother at the age of 26 years old. It was so dark outside, and rain was coming down so hard that it was burning my eyes; just trying to focus and keep the car straight on the road. I wondered if I was doing the right thing leaving our good friends and my children's grandmother and moving so far away to a place where we did not know anyone. I finally saw a motel ahead with its flashing sign that read vacancy, and I put my blinker on and pulled the car into the right lane to get off the highway. I stopped, woke the girls, and went in to get a room.

I carried their sleepy little bodies struggling to open the office door and saw a man come running to my rescue. "You have your hands full young lady," he said, smiling while opening the door for me. "Yes, do you have a room for the night? The storm is getting so bad that it is hard for me to see the road anymore," I told him. He set me up with a room, gave me the key, helped me with my small overnight bag, and led me down the hallway to our room. I thanked him and said goodnight. I laid the girls down on one of the beds and tucked them in. They immediately fell back to sleep. I looked at their innocent, sleeping faces, and tears came to my eyes as I thought how much they both looked like their daddy. It wasn't fair that they would never know him, I thought. I lay down on the bed next to them and fell asleep.

The following day, I woke early to the girls giggling next to me. I rubbed my sleepy eyes and looked up at them, chattering amongst each other, and I grabbed them both up in a bear hug. I changed their clothes, got them ready for the day, cleaned myself up, and we all checked out to start our adventure again. I was grateful that it was no longer raining, and the sun was beginning to come out, making it a peaceful, warm morning.

We continued our journey after I fed the girls some breakfast. I decided to drive approximately 6 hours a day, stopping to rest at motels and trying to give the girls some fun times along the way. I told Carrie that we were going on an adventure to find our dream home, and she was excited about it, but the drive was also long and tiresome.

We pulled into Springfield, Wisconsin, late afternoon on June 25, 1990. The girls were cranky and tired of being in a car. I was scared to death of failing as a mother. I was scared of being alone and scared of not being able to meet people and build a life without Mike, but I shrugged off my negative thoughts and pulled up in front of the house where I was supposed to meet the realtor. I had called him in advance and scheduled a showing. He arrived a bit late, so I sat in the car and gave the kids a snack while we waited for the realtor to arrive. When he came, I let Carrie out of her car seat and unbuckled Jenni to carry her in. He showed us around, and I immediately fell in love with the house.

I made an offer, and he made one phone call and turned to us after he had hung up. "It's yours," he said quickly. He had kind eyes, and I trusted him when he told me about the neighborhood and the house. "The neighborhood is quiet, but a few kids live on the block and down the street. You will like it here. The people are friendly and very accepting and helpful. It's a very close nit town, and the people will welcome you with open arms." He told me. "If you are interested, the local paper is looking for an office assistant with some photography skills." He said as he shook my hand and collected my earnest money for the house. "Thank you, I am very interested," I told him. I will go there first thing in the morning, I thought to myself.

We stayed in another motel that night, but the following morning I could move into our new home, and the moving truck came with our belongings right on time. It was such a small town that I was able to move into the home before completing all of the paperwork. The house was only $62,800, and I was able to put down a check in the amount of $30,000, so they were pleased with the down payment and allowed us to have the keys immediately. As I was unpacking our belongings and hanging things up, the doorbell rang, and I ran to answer it before it woke the girls up from their afternoon nap.

"Hi, neighbor," a woman shrieked and reached out her hand to shake mine. I shook her hand. "I am Cathy, and I live right next door to you. If you need anything, holler anytime." Her voice was full of energy, and she talked so fast. I smiled and nodded. "Come in" I stood back so she could pass by me. "I'm Kally; it's nice to meet you, Cathy," I told her. "I am part of the Springfield Jaycees, and we do a lot of volunteer work for the town; plus, I am also head of the welcoming committee for newcomers to our town. We would love it if you joined our committee. We always seek new ideas and help to better our little community." She stood there smiling and chattering away, twirling her long red hair and looking bubbly.

Cathy was very petite and looked to be around 30 years old. She had beautiful blue eyes that sparkled when she spoke. She seemed to be very comfortable and confident when she spoke, but she sputtered her words quickly and was so full of energy that it was hard to keep up with what she was saying. "Slow down!" I said, holding one hand up. "I have had a long journey and am slow in my thought process." I laughed, and she stopped with wide eyes and laughed too. 'Well, I have to run, it was very nice meeting you, Kally, and I will talk to you soon." She spoke. I nodded and closed the door behind her, thinking that Cathy and I would become great friends whether I liked it or not. I smiled and thought it would be okay because I already liked her.

That night I made supper for the kids, and I put them to bed early so I could relax from my exhausting day of unpacking and settling in. I looked around at my home and realized I had accomplished a considerable amount in one day. The curtains were all hanging up, the clothes were all put away, and I only had a few boxes left to unpack. I glanced at the big box next to the dining room table and gasped for air. It was Mike's box of things that he had saved growing up. I picked up the box, carried it to the basement, and tucked it under the stairs. I couldn't bring myself to go through it, and I thought maybe it would be okay if I saved it under the steps for our children when they were old enough to have it.

I fell asleep in the chair that night watching television and woke up the following morning to Jenni crying for me. I ran to her rescue, changed her quickly, and brought her to her highchair for breakfast. I set some Cheerios on her tray to tide her over until I could cook up some scrambled eggs and bacon. As I was cooking, Carrie woke up and joined us in the kitchen. She came to me with sleepy eyes and wrapped her arms around me for her morning hug.

I kissed her on the cheek and set her at the table for breakfast. As we were finishing up our breakfast, the doorbell rang.

I quickly washed up my hands, grabbed a towel to dry them off, and tried to get to the door, but Carrie ran to the door before I could get there and swung it open in delightful hellos. I rushed to her side and pulled her back by my legs like a mama bear protecting her cub. A man in a dark blue uniform stood at my door. I looked at the name tag on his shirt and saw that he was a heating and air conditioning repairman.

"Hi, miss, I am Jesse Baker." He reached out to shake my hand. "Mel and Jamie told me that I am supposed to fix your Air conditioning unit." I recognized the names as being the previous owners of the house. "Oh yes, they said that they would have that fixed," I said, shaking his hand. I remembered that it was part of our agreement on the house to have the air conditioning unit up and running. I showed him to the basement where the furnace was and opened the box on the front of the furnace. "I will just grab my tools then and get to work." He told me. He brushed past me and went to his truck. I went back to the girls in the kitchen.

In a couple of hours, I could no longer hear clanking and banging in the basement. I was settling Jenni down for her morning nap and putting Carrie on the couch to watch cartoons when Jesse came up with his toolbox in his right hand and a smile on his face. "All fixed." He announced. I smiled and thanked him. He stood in front of me with his big brown eyes smiling at me. His warm and friendly smile comforted me and made me blush a little. He was tall and lean, wearing a dark blue tank that showed his tanned, muscular shoulders.

He had a tinge of sweat lining his dark brown hair that was a little too long from the men I was used to seeing on the army base. He suddenly broke the silence and brought my thoughts back to reality when he turned to Carrie and said, "That has got to be one of my favorite cartoons in the world," Carrie was giggling on the couch to one of her favorite Tom and Jerry cartoons.

I kept staring at Jesse as he quickly bonded with my little girl. She looked up at him and started her little chatter, and he kept

talking to her, making her feel important as she explained how the cartoon went. Suddenly I felt a pang of guilt rush through me, and immediately,
I jumped in front of Jesse and told him rudely that we had a busy day planned.

"Hey, sorry to keep you," he apologized and started for the door. "I am sorry for being rude; it's just that….." My voice broke, and I stopped. Jesse patted my arm gently, "It's okay, Kally; I will talk to you later." He told me and shut the door behind him. I opened the door quickly and yelled out, "Thanks again, Jesse, and it was nice meeting you" He looked back and waved goodbye with a warm and friendly smile.

Minutes later, Cathy was at my door, she came in, and we talked over coffee for a couple of hours. I then asked her if she could watch the girls for me while I ran uptown to apply for the job at the newspaper, and she agreed. "Is it okay if I take the girls to the park, and you can just meet us over there after your interview?" She asked as Carrie jumped up and down, yelling, "Yes! Please, Mommy!" I agreed and grabbed my purse, and left for town.

The newspaper office was easy to find as I drove down the main street; the storefront had, in big letters across the top of the building, "Springfield News and Clues." I walked in and asked for an application, and the woman at the counter told me to wait there and that she would get Sam. I didn't know who Sam was, but I assumed he must be her supervisor. Minutes later, a short, chunky man in his early 60s came up to the counter with his hand outstretched to me.

"Hi, I am Kally" I reached out to shake his hand. "I have just moved to town, and I am in desperate need of a job quickly. I have minimal experience in photography but did a little in high school, and I can type rather quickly and take phone messages. I also am a quick learner and would love it if you would give me a chance to prove myself." He held up his hand, and I realized I was babbling as quickly as Cathy. I was sure he wouldn't hire me for my sheer desperation, but instead, he asked, "When can you start, Kally?"

I shrieked, "Really? You are giving me the job?" He laughed and nodded, "Welcome aboard, Kally." I bolted towards him and hugged him, "Thank you, thank you, I promise! You will not be sorry." He stepped back, and I released my clutch on him, apologizing for manhandling him. He thought it was amusing as he laughed.

I told him I could start as soon as I found suitable daycare for my children. He quickly jotted down names and numbers and told me to call these people for daycare. "This one especially, I like," he said as he pointed to the name that read "Cuddly Character's Daycare." I liked the name and called them as soon as I left his office. A young woman on the phone answered, and I could hear children chattering all kinds of noises in the background. Her name was Pam, and she told me I could come right over to meet her and gave me directions.

I pulled up in her driveway, and she had a large fenced-in yard with a vast assortment of toys, swings, slides, and a sandbox. Pam answered the door with a baby on her hip and reached out her hand. I shook her hand and told her my name. "I have two little girls, Carrie is 3 1/2, and Jenni is 11 months old," I told her.

"I have room for both of them," she replied, motioning for me to come in to show me around. Pam told me the schedule she kept with the children and showed me what she does to run a somewhat smooth household. She has two children of her own, too, ages 4 and 2, both boys. Her hands were full, but she looked like she loved spending time with children, and her patience was remarkable. I stayed there visiting for about an hour and watched her as she put lunch on the table for about eight children, all under the age of 6. I was impressed with her and her home, so I agreed to start the girls there in the morning.

I ran back to tell Sam that I could begin work in the morning. He seemed pleased with my enthusiasm and told me he would start me at $6.00 per hour. I was thrilled, as it was above minimum wage, and it also had some benefits offered as well. I left excited to tell Cathy my good news. I parked the car in front of the small park and glanced around until I saw Cathy sitting on the park bench with

Jenni in her lap. I walked up and heard Carrie call out, "Watch me, Mommy" I looked over, and she was going down the slide. I waved and smiled at her and sat down next to Cathy on the bench.

Cathy was thrilled when I told her about the job, and she also talked me into joining the Springfield Jaycees. They had an upcoming fundraiser coming up in August. "Can you make cookies and make some posters to hang up?" She asked. I agreed and worked on posters in my spare time for the next two weeks. I met many people, it seemed, in such a short time while working at the newspaper. They all seemed so welcoming that it took my mind off the loss of my husband during the day. That was precisely my intention. I thought if I poured myself into so many activities, I wouldn't have time to think about anything else.

Then nighttime would fall, all the memories were fresh on my mind, and the tears would come again. I missed Mike so much and wondered If I would ever sleep a whole night without him by my side again. Carrie asked me on occasion about her daddy, but soon she stopped asking and seemed to have forgotten all about him. She was so young, and I was jealous that the girls could wipe their little minds from the pain of losing their daddy. I sometimes wished I could forget as well, but then again, I would not have the cherished memories of the love I felt for those years I had with him, and I didn't want to give those memories up for nothing.

I finally dozed off to sleep and awoke to the alarm clock ringing at 6 am. I put some coffee on and sat down at the kitchen table to write a list of things I needed to get for the house. I wanted to paint a couple of rooms in the house and get some new curtains to brighten the place up. The living room was a mint green color that I didn't care for, and I thought I would paint that room burgundy on one wall and an olive color on the remaining four walls to match my olive-colored furniture. The girls' bedroom was painted yellow, and I thought I would paint that room lavender and pink to match their polka-dotted curtains.

The house was very open throughout, which drew me to it right away. The front door was a beautiful white door with an arc glass etched in gold, and when you entered the house from there, you entered a large foyer. The living room was off to the right with a big archway. It stepped down two steps to a sunken living room and two steps up on the other side to the dining room with windows surrounding it, letting in all the sunlight. The kitchen was open to the dining room, separated by an Island breakfast bar. The cabinetry was a golden oak color with gold handles. Many cabinets surrounded every wall, and a pantry was in the corner of the kitchen. The window over the sink overlooked our large backyard with a swing set already in place and a sizeable homemade sandbox.

The yard was completely fenced in and had two large oak trees and one apple tree in the back. The bedrooms were down the hall, opposite the foyer, and a primary bathroom with a jacuzzi sitting in the corner and a shower in the other corner. Both bedrooms had a walk-in closet and were large rooms. Right off the kitchen was a large laundry room where I set up my washer and dryer and still had room for a table to fold the clothes on. I loved that everything was on one level, but I also loved that there was a basement to use for a storm shelter.

The basement still needed to be finished, and it was only a half basement, which I found bizarre, but came in handy for a storm shelter and storage. It was one large room that entered straight ahead of the foyer. The room was a concrete floor, but the walls were sheet-rocked and taped. I could paint that room to brighten it up as well. The front yard had a nice deck off the front, just like Ali's house, and I thought I could buy a swing to set out there for when she came to visit us, she could swing and feel like she was at home.

The yard had a wide assortment of beautiful flowers, shrubs, and flowering trees. I knew the woman who lived here before I bought it must have loved to be outside planting. In the backyard, there was a large area for a garden that needed to see a tiller before spring planting, but of course it was too late in the season to do anything with it this year. Next year, I could have a lovely garden to keep me busy. The girls would be old enough to help and love digging in the dirt and planting vegetables and flowers.

I went to shower after a couple of cups of coffee. I then put on my makeup, fixed up my hair, put on a nice outfit that I thought would look nice for the office, and then went to get the girls ready to bring them to daycare. Pam invited me in for a cup of coffee when I arrived at daycare.

I had a few minutes to spare, and I wanted the girls to feel comfortable with me leaving, so I accepted her invitation and went in. I removed the girls' jackets, and they immediately joined in with the other children playing, laughing, and listening to some children's music. They seemed to fit right in, which reassured me that they would be okay there while I was at work.

Pam told me that she had been doing daycare for so many years that she was unsure she could do anything else. She also told me that I was going to like it in Springfield. She said 90% of the people here were sincerely friendly and trustworthy. "The other 10%, just don't talk to them," she laughed as she picked up a crying toddler and cuddled him in close.

I told her to have a nice day, hugged Carrie and Jenni, told them I would be back soon, and to be good for Pam. They giggled and went back to playing. That was easy, I thought to myself. I looked back before I left, and Jenni was sitting on the floor playing with blocks, and Carrie was playing with another little girl with the child's kitchen set and dishes. I smiled again and told Pam to have a great day.

The first day at the office was mostly training, and Sam took the time to point out everything carefully. I took notes so I wouldn't forget, and before I knew it, the noon whistle was blowing through town. "Lunchtime," Sam announced as he grabbed his keys, and everyone in the office got up to follow. "Oh," I said. "How long is lunch break?" I asked. "One hour, do you want to go with us to the café down the street? They have amazing home-cooked meals." He boasted. I agreed and followed towards the door, grabbing my purse on the way out.

Sam locked up behind us, and we all walked to the café. The sign on the front had big Red and Black lettering that read "Mindy's Grub." What a name for a restaurant, I thought. Springfield was definitely a small town; I laughed to myself.

Sam was right, though; the food was excellent. I ordered the Fish fillet lunch, and it came with a large fillet of fish, real homemade mashed potatoes and gravy, and a generous portion of corn. I couldn't eat everything on my plate, or I would have had to nap before returning to work, so I asked for a to-go box to put in the refrigerator at work and take it home for supper.

Rose came with us to the café as well. She was the receptionist at the office. She was in her late fifties and a rather large woman with long hair that she let go gray. I wondered why she wouldn't cut some of that hair and get a lovely updo hairstyle, but I guess that is how she liked it. She didn't talk a lot, and I wondered if she was just quiet or didn't like me, but I tried to make small talk with her anyway. On the other hand, Sam was very talkative and controlled much of the conversation at the table.

The café was starting to fill up, and we were finishing our lunch when I looked up and saw the heating and air conditioning man come inside with a group of guys. I remembered his name was Jesse. He saw me, smiled, and raised his hand to give me a wave. I nodded his way and smiled back, trying not to look like I was excited to see him. He was very good-looking, and I couldn't help myself to glance his way once or twice, but then extreme guilt would rush over me as I thought of my husband, whom I had just buried three months ago. How could I even be looking at another man? I thought, disgusted with myself.

Sam took the check to the register, put his hand up to my protest, and paid the bill. I thanked him for lunch, grabbed my purse, and started for the door. "How's that AC been working for you?" a deep voice came from behind me. I turned face to face with Jesse and slightly blushed at his presence next to me. "It works great," I replied, not knowing what else to say. I quickly stammered for more words, "How are you?" I asked, sounding nervous and clumsy. He smiled. "I'm fine, Kally.

Do you plan on attending the dance this Friday?" Before I could answer him, he asked if I would like to go with him. I immediately felt the blood rush to my head and swayed to the side, feeling dizzy. He caught my arm, "Are you okay?" He asked with a worried line across his forehead. "I'm fine; I have to go back to work, Jesse; sorry, I will talk to you later," I said quickly and practically ran out the door, leaving him standing there confused.

What was wrong with me, I thought to myself. I couldn't betray my husband and be interested in another man. It was way too soon, yet I felt a connection to Jesse that I couldn't explain. I decided to wipe it from my mind and get back to work. I would have to focus on working, caring for my girls, and staying far away from this man. I thought my life was no longer my own, and I had to make my girls the center of my universe. Yes, they would keep me so busy that I didn't need any other distractions in my life to lead me down the wrong path.

CHAPTER SIX

GOING THROUGH THE MOTIONS

I came across a flyer at the bank advertising an event involving kids and parents. I decided to write the number down and give them a call. It was a parent/child group at the community center. I decided to join so the girls would meet more kids from town, and I would also meet other moms. The classes were held at the Community center every Tuesday at 6 pm. I decided to start the following Tuesday. I told the girls about it, and Carrie was excited to try something new. She heard kids and toys, and they were all for it. We arrived a few minutes before 6 pm, and only three other moms were there with their children.

Many stations were set up for the kids to play with playdough, coloring books, building blocks, water activities, and synthetic sand. I was pushing Jenni in her stroller, and Carrie was tugging at my hand to go faster to the fun activities. It was a little overwhelming, which must have shown because a short, bubbly, dark-haired lady came to my rescue. She introduced herself as Wendy, my neighbor down the street. She told Carrie to go over to that table and pointed to the play dough table. "My daughter, Sara is behind the table to help you build lots of fun things," Wendy said, smiling. Carrie looked at me for approval, and I told her to go ahead. "Mommy will be right over here," I pointed to a bench off to the side where some other ladies were sitting.

Wendy and I chatted for a while, and she introduced me to some of the other ladies. A few more moms came in later, and we visited, played with the kids, and then began cleaning up the mess. It was a group to vent about your stresses in child rearing, meet other parents going through some of the same things, and spend bonding time with your children. I met a few more people from town, and the girls had fun playing with the other children. I was glad I joined the group; it gave me quality time with my kids and time out of the house. Another bonus about the group is that when we arrived home, the girls were exhausted, and our bedtime ritual was easy. They didn't even make it through a story and were fast asleep.

Friday came, and I decided to make an appearance at the dance to get out of the house for one night. I called the neighbor girl, Sara, to come and babysit, and she quickly agreed. She was a thin girl with red hair and freckles on her cheeks. She had two dimples on the right side of her cheek, which were hard to miss when she smiled. The girls liked Sara immediately when they met her at the Parent/child group we attended, and she seemed to hit it off with them quite well from the start.

She wasn't shy and talked so quickly that I had to ask her to repeat herself on several occasions, but she was funny, sweet, and always willing to lend a helping hand with the girls whenever I needed her. She arrived at 7 pm sharp, and I decided to walk uptown to the dance just in case I decided to have a couple of drinks; I didn't want to be driving.

I finished applying my makeup and threw on a pair of my favorite jeans and a white blouse. I topped it off with dangly earrings and my pearl necklace choker around my neck. I left my hair flowing down with a few loose curls around the ends, and I took one final look in the mirror and decided I looked good enough. I walked in through the front doors of the community center and paid my entrance fee of $3.00 at the door, and walked into a loud chattering room. When I arrived, the band was on break, and I saw Sam sitting with his wife, Ella.

I walked over to say hello, and Sam introduced me as the new girl in the office. Ella shook my hand, "It is nice meeting you; Sam tells me that you moved here from California?" she asked, starting a small conversation. Sam got up to pull out my chair and motioned for me to sit down. Ella was easygoing and pleasant to talk to. She seemed to like talking, so I listened attentively and answered her questions. She made it easy for me to feel comfortable in the conversation. A few other people joined us at the table, and Sam quickly introduced me to all of them, being careful not to leave me out. I could tell he was very kind and caring, and he went out of his way to make others feel comfortable, and I liked that he and his wife had those traits. They both knew everyone in town and seemed to get along with everyone. They were not the type of people to talk badly about anyone and were involved in many community activities and fundraising.

Ella had light blondish-gray hair that was permed and fixed up perfectly. She wore a lot of jewelry and a ring on almost every finger. Her lipstick was bright red, and her makeup was flawlessly applied. I concluded that Ella liked feeling beautiful, and her apparent kindness showed her true beauty. I later found out that Sam used to be the town Mayor but retired from that position when his youngest daughter passed away in a car accident three years ago. He decided to retire to help Ella and their young son, Brody, through the grieving and loss. It was extremely devastating for all of them. Cathy told me that Ella had therapy afterward and that she had a slight nervous breakdown. I thought to myself. I couldn't imagine going through something like that. That would be the most painful, tragic experience ever to go through.

A couple of the gals at the table, Bonnie and Tammi, asked me to come out and dance with them, and I did. It was fun, and I was glad I had decided to attend the dance. Around 10 pm, I was out on the dance floor having a great time dancing when I spotted Jesse across the room standing next to the bar with a blonde girl on his arm. She was snuggled close to him. She looked a little older than him and was a lot shorter too. Her hair was thrown up in a messy ponytail, and she had a shirt that showed a little too much belly. If I sound jealous, I was. He looked my way then and caught me staring at them, and I quickly turned away. I walked off the dance floor to get a drink.

I ordered a vodka sour and fumbled for my money to pay the bartender when a hand with a five-dollar bill slipped in front of me, "I got it," Jesse's voice came from behind me. I twirled around to face him, "Thank you, but you didn't have to do that," I told him. "I know I didn't have to, but I wanted to, Kally, if that's okay?" He smiled.

"Well, thank you," I said again. I sipped on my drink and began to walk back to the table, but Jesse stayed by my side, walking, "Are you having a good time?" He touched my arm to stop me, and I was afraid the goosebumps that formed on my arms were visible. I stopped and looked at him, "I am having a nice time, yes. Who is your date?" I asked.

He smiled at my curiosity, leaned closer to me, and with a whispery voice, replied, "She's my neighbor, and she asked me to take her to the dance." He told me in a highly flirtatious, sexy voice. "Oh well, I wouldn't want to keep you from your date," I told him to have a great time and quickly walked away before he could stop me. I shot a look back toward him, and he was still standing there watching me with a puzzled grin on his face. I returned to the table, grabbed my purse, and made excuses as to why I had to get home.

I practically ran out the door and started walking home when I heard footsteps behind me. I twirled around, startled to find Jesse running to catch up with me. "What is wrong, Kally?" He said with a stern but worried look on his face. "Nothing, go back to your date; I am just going home." I snapped. He reached out and touched my arm, "Did I do something to offend you?" He still had that worried look. "Oh, no. I just…" I could not tell him that the very presence of him around me made my body want to go into convulsions. "I just have to get home to the girls." I lied. "Kally, it's only 11 o'clock. I am sure they are fine and sleeping." He assured me.

He then took my hand and tried to pull me in the other direction, "Come for a walk with me; let's talk." He demanded politely, still pulling me. I could tell he was not going to let me protest, and I honestly didn't want to. My insides were full of butterflies, and my head told me to run for cover. He tugged again, and I nodded okay.

We walked down by the park, and Jesse, still holding my hand firmly, led me to the bench, and we sat down and talked. He told me that he had grown up in Springfield, and his parents died when he was 15 years old, so he lived with his grandparents. His grandpa passed away a couple of years ago, and he only had his grandmother left. She lived in the nursing home in town now, and he visited her every Sunday afternoon.

He told me that he has one older sister, Sherri, who lives on the south side of town with her husband, Frank, whom she dated in high school and married right after graduation. They have three children, two girls and one boy, ages 8, 6, and 4 years old. Jesse told me he also has two children with his ex-wife, Laurie. Two girls, 3 and 5 years old, Jessica and Bella. He sees them every weekend, and they spend the night at his house whenever they like. He told me that they have a very open child visitation schedule and mostly leave it up to the kids to decide when they want to go to their dad's and when they want to go to their mom's house.

"It works great right now, and it stops everyone from fighting over the kids. I also help her with whatever she needs, and we are still friends, making it easier for everyone". He told me. He said he dated Laurie in high school, and she became pregnant with Jess. He decided that marriage was the best option. When he asked, she said yes, so they both went to the courthouse and were married immediately before the baby arrived. He was 22 years old, and Laurie was 19.

"Neither one of us was ready for marriage nor a baby, but when she arrived, I fell in love with her instantly. I just wish it could have been that way with Laurie and me," He said sadly. "We divorced shortly after Bella was born, but it was a mutually agreed split, and we both remained great friends." Then he turned towards me, taking my hand again, "Now tell me about you; what brings you to town?" He asked.

"I closed my eyes and pointed to a place on my map, and this is the town that I chose," I told him. "You're kidding, right?" He laughed. "I am serious!" I told him sternly.

"Why did you leave wherever you came from?" He pried further. I jumped to my feet when my eyes welled up with tears, "I have to go home," I shrieked louder than I wanted to. He grabbed my hand and stopped me. "I am sorry, Kally; I didn't mean to pry," He had that worried look on his face again, and he reached and brushed the hair that had fallen on my face as I looked at the ground. With one hand under my chin, he gently lifted my face to look at him.

"I'm sorry, whatever is hurting you, I am truly sorry." His face was so gentle and loving that I could tell he was deeply concerned. "No, I am sorry," I told him. "It is just so hard right now; I mean, I am trying to move forward and forget everything; I mean, I, I...." My voice was broken, and my eyes were full of tears. Jesse pulled me towards him and wrapped his arms around me, and held me close to him as I broke down and cried hysterically.

I let everything out that I had been holding in for months and let him comfort me. He sat me back on the bench, and when I finally felt like I had no tears left to cry, I pulled myself together and told Jesse everything. I told him how I met Mike, how wonderful he was, and what a great life we had together. I told him I felt cheated when God took him from me so soon and quickly, not letting me even say Goodbye to him.

I told him I was angry at God for taking this beautiful man away from my children and me. I told him everything, and he listened to me without saying anything until I was completely finished. He then lifted my chin again and said, "I am so sorry for your loss Kally." "I think it is truly unique, though, that you had almost four years of such powerful love in your life, and I just wonder why you want to forget that?" He had such wonder in his eyes and concern.

"I never thought of it like that," I told him. "I just thought that if I could forget it all, the pain would go away." He wiped the tears from my eyes and held me next to him again. "The pain will ease after time, and you will have good memories of him to tell your girls so that they will also know the man that you knew and loved so much," He whispered gently and brushed his lips to my forehead.

Jesse was warm and sensitive, yet he looked rugged and strong. I felt warm and safe in his arms and didn't want to let go of him. He walked me home, turned to me in front of my house, leaned forward, and kissed me gently on the cheek, but I felt so much passion in that kiss. "Good night, Kally; call me at this number if you would like to talk more." He said as he handed me a business card with his number on it. "Thanks for lending an ear and a shoulder," I said, smiling up into his beautiful brown eyes. "Anytime," he winked and walked back down the walk.

I watched him fade into the dark shadows down the block. The next day I called Jesse, and I was relieved that he didn't answer and I could leave a voice mail. I told him that I was sorry for unloading my problems on him the night before and that I thought it was best that we don't see each other anymore. I told him that I had to focus on raising my daughters and giving everything I could to improve their lives, and any distractions would not be fair to them. I also told him that I wasn't ready to let another man into my life again and that it wouldn't be acceptable to lead him on in any way. I hung up the phone and hoped he would understand and not call me back.

A couple of days passed when I got a phone call from him. He told me he understood how I felt and respected my boundaries, but he refused to avoid me. "It's a small town, Kally, and we are going to run into each other, so I don't see why we can't be friends." He assured me that there was no harm in that, and I reluctantly agreed.

One morning after a good night's sleep, I awoke to Carrie by my bedside demanding breakfast. I put my feet on the floor, feeling revived and brighter than I had felt all year. I went to get Jenni out of her crib, changed her, and brought her to the kitchen to set her in her highchair. I made the girls waffles with my Mickey Mouse waffle iron, singing softly while I was stirring the batter. I could hear the girls giggling, and I turned to see them giggling at me as they watched me singing cheerfully.

"What so funny" I ran over to Jenni and tickled her belly, and she squealed with delight. "Tickle me too, Mamma," Carrie pleaded. I ran around the table to her toes and tickled them, and both girls laughed. "Let's get dressed and go to the Park," I shrieked, and Carrie began yelling, "Get ready, get ready!" Jenni screamed out in delight. I packed a light lunch of snacks to take along with us, and I grabbed a blanket and a book for me to read while they played with the other kids on the playground.

I loaded the girls in the car, and we were off to the park for the day, or at least until after lunch, and then we would come back to take a nice little cozy nap; that was my plan for the day. We had lived in Springfield for almost a year, and with Carrie starting preschool in the fall, I wanted to enjoy the rest of the summer, giving the girls quality time with me.

I found a nice shady spot under a beautiful, tall oak tree, and I laid the blanket out and placed the picnic basket on the corner of the blanket to secure it down. The sun was shining brightly and warm out, so I put some sunscreen on the girls. Carrie ran off to the swings, and Jenni sat with me on the blanket with some toys. I didn't feel much like reading yet, so I played with Jenni while keeping a close eye on Carrie playing with all the other little children, laughing, and having fun like they didn't have a care in the world.

I grabbed my camera from my purse and began to take a few pictures of their happy faces running and playing so excitedly. I took Jenni by the hand, led her to the swing set, put her in the toddler swing, and began pushing her. I snapped a few more pictures. Wouldn't it be nice to see the world through the eyes of a child? I thought. So innocent and trusting of all things, all people. They haven't yet been tattered and worn in their lifetime, and I wish I could protect them and keep their innocence alive for as long as possible.

After they were done swinging, I lay on my blanket and watched as Carrie played on the slides and Jenni was in the sandbox playing with some toys I had brought along. Carrie would slide down the slide and then run over to Jenni and act silly so that Jenni would giggle. I smiled with pride at how Carrie and Jenni played so nicely together. They never fought over toys or whined about the other getting more than them. Carrie always seemed like she watched out for Jenni, and it was nice to see that Carrie didn't mind sharing with Jenni, even when Jenni was a bit demanding and grabbed the toys out of Carrie's hands. Carrie was patient with her. The sound of rustling leaves behind me startled me and brought me back from my thoughts,

"Hey, Sexy lady!" A familiar voice came from behind. I spun around, and there stood Jesse. "Hi" I tried to act like my heart wasn't pounding out of my chest at the very sight of him. "What are you doing here?" I asked him. He pointed to 2 little kids playing in the sandbox.

"Those little beauties are mine." He proudly announced. I noticed his girls when they jumped in the sandbox, but I did not know that they were Jesse's girls. My girls came running over to the blanket and plopped down, announcing that they were hungry, so I took out some sandwiches and chips.

Jesse sat on the blanket next to me, and we talked as the girls ate lunch. Jesse's two girls came running over next, and I asked if they wanted a sandwich. They smiled and nodded quickly. "You don't have to feed my kids your lunch, Kally." Jesse smiled. "I brought enough to feed the whole park," I told him and laughed. "Do you want one too?" He smiled at me and reached out to accept the sandwich I held up and brushed against my hand. I pulled back quickly so that he would overlook the attraction that I had for him.

We ran into each other from time to time, and we became good friends in passing, but whenever Jesse seemed like he wanted more, I found an excuse to shut him down. I told the kids to eat up quickly because it was time to go home.

Jesse asked what the hurry was, and I told him I was going home to get some things done around the house before the work week started again. "Let's take the kids to the Drive Inn movie next weekend. I want to spend more time with you, Kally, and …" I stopped him from going on and put my hand up.

"I am not ready to get involved with anyone, Jesse; I am sorry, but I think it is best that we don't go to a movie." I quickly started packing up the basket and rolling up the blanket. I told the kids to put their sandals back on. They protested, but I gave them a look so that they knew I was not backing down and that it was time to go.

"I thought that you and I were becoming friends, Kally?" He looked like I had hit him over the head. "Jesse, I like you, and I believe you are a great guy, but I have to focus on raising my girls alone and working. I don't need distractions right now." I explained.

I didn't want my words to sound so cold, but I also didn't want Jesse to look into my eyes and see that I was lying to him, either. I couldn't let him know that being close to him sent chills throughout my body, and I couldn't let him see how much he excited me and how

I wanted to be with him in more ways than he knew. It was best that I break all ties with him and steer clear of him so that these feelings would pass. I didn't want to betray Mike this way, and I still felt married to my beloved husband, that would never return to me.

He reached for his children's hands, and with an obvious hurt and disappointed look on his face, he told me to take care, and he walked away. It broke my heart to lie to him, but I thought I was doing the right thing. We were both lonely, and a relationship can't be built on that; I kept telling myself. I stayed busy at work and with the kids for the next few weeks. I began painting more and fixing things up around the house. I opened a savings account in town and decided to save enough money to take the girls to see their grandma, Ali, around Christmas time. I wouldn't tell them now, though; I would surprise them. I made sure that I talked about her to them all the time, and I let them speak to her on the phone at least once a week so they wouldn't forget her. I also called their aunt Maggie, and we chatted with her often. I didn't want the girls to ever forget that side of their family.

By the end of the summer, I had saved up enough money to take a quick weekend trip to see Ali and Maggie. I decided I didn't want to wait until Christmas. I called Ali on the phone to ensure they both would be home and set my plan in motion. She was so excited; I heard her shriek loudly over the phone as she told Maggie we were coming for a visit. It was only a couple hour drive in the car, and it was imperative that we stay in closer touch. When we arrived on Friday late afternoon, she came out to greet us with her warm hugs. The girls giggled as Ali pinched their cheeks and told them how much they had grown.

"I have some fresh, warm chocolate chip cookies in the house for you girls." She announced, and the girls ran for the door. That night after tucking the girls into bed, I sat down with Ali and Maggie and updated them on what was going on in our lives. I told them about my job and how friendly the people from Springfield were; I told them about Cathy and what a great friend she had become. I left out the part about meeting Jesse and how he made me feel whenever I saw him.

I didn't want Ali and Maggie to feel like I had forgotten about Mike because I didn't. It was just loneliness that I felt. It was a lovely visit, but way too short, I thought as I began loading the girls in the car, saying our goodbyes. "I will be back sooner next time," I promised as I started my drive back to Springfield with tears in my eyes. Ali and Maggie promised they would plan a trip to come and see us too.

CHAPTER SEVEN

STAYING BUSY

I woke up one Saturday afternoon, and the house felt colder than usual. It was time to turn the heat on. Winter was just around the bend, and fall was short-lived in Wisconsin., It was time to start getting ready for the colder months and pull out all our warmer clothing. I began unpacking a few things and threw a bunch of hats, mittens, and jackets in the washing machine. I went out to the backyard, loaded up all the sandbox toys, and brought them into the house to wash them up. Then I went out to cover the rose bushes planted in the backyard before moving in. I wanted to make sure that I took care of all the beautiful flowers and plants that someone put a great deal of their time into planting and making everything look so wonderful in the yard.

Jesse had tried several times to call me, but I let my voicemail pick it up. He left messages telling me he missed me and to call him back. Still, I thought it was best to stay away until I was strong enough to be around him without feeling the intense passion I felt whenever he brushed against me. I was a complete mess by lunchtime, and the girls didn't look any better as they followed me around the yard, copying me and playing in the dirt every chance they got. I decided it was time to go in and get cleaned up for lunch when I noticed Jesse's truck pull up in the driveway. My heart started beating faster, and I immediately tried to smooth my messy hair.

He got out of the truck and came towards me. I hadn't seen him since the day in the park over two months ago, and I wondered if something was wrong. "Jesse, is everything okay?" I asked. Looking a little confused, he said, "Sam called me and told me your furnace is broken" My eyebrows raised up in confusion as well, "Nothing seems to be wrong with my furnace, I turned it on this morning, and it works fine," I told him. Suddenly it dawned on me that my boss was trying to play matchmaker, and I shook my head, frustrated and upset with Sam. "I am sorry, Jesse; I didn't know Sam was going to do this," I told him.

Jesse smiled his sexy little grin, "Well, it's nice to see you anyway, Kally. I am glad your furnace is working properly. How are you?" he asked, trying to make conversation in a very awkward moment. "I am good; I have been busy getting the house fixed up and now getting things put away for the winter months. "I am a mess," I said, holding my dirty hands up to show him. He put his right hand on my cheek and wiped some dirt away, "You look beautiful, Kally, as always" he smiled that sexy grin at me, and my heart beat a little faster. I backed up a step and quickly pulled myself together. "How are your kids?" I asked, changing the subject. He must have taken it as a brush-off again because his smile faded from his face, and he quickly said they were doing fine and said he had to get back to work. He was back in his truck and sped down the road without looking back.

I stood there with a sick feeling in my stomach and tears in my eyes. "I could slap Sam for doing this," I thought. "How could he?" I took the girls in the house and got cleaned up for lunch, thinking that I would call Sam tonight and let him know that it was wrong of him to call Jesse and tell him to mind his own business. When Sam answered the phone that evening, I was very short with him and let him know that he shouldn't ever do that again, and he listened to my every word before he finally spoke.

"Are you finished now, Kally?" he asked. "YES," I yelled into the phone. "Good! I am sorry that I told Jesse that, but you need to get out of the house and join the living girl," he continued before I could object. "You stay cooped up in that house and spend all your waking hours either at work or with the children, and you need to get out and spend time with friends and live a little" he paused for a second for my reaction. "I appreciate your concern Sam, but I am fine! I just got back from a trip to see the girl's grandmother," I snapped and ordered him to stay out of my business firmly but politely. "Sorry, Kally. I was only trying to help," he replied. "I know, but really I am fine," I lied.

If I had told him the truth, I would have told him how lonely I was and how I longed for a man's arms around me, holding me close at night again and falling asleep in a man's arms again is what I truly missed, but I felt guilty for even thinking like that. I had my chance at love and my one and only true love, but he had to go away for some reason that I am so angry about and so full of resentment because of it. I still didn't understand why my perfect life had to change, but it did, and now my primary purpose in life was raising my girls and making their lives as happy as I could possibly make them. My social life didn't exist without the girls in it. We went to our fun nights, I socialized with other parents, and I joined my co-workers for lunch. As far as a social life without my children, I didn't have one, and I didn't think it was necessary to have one either.

Months went by, and winter came and went. The snow on the ground was melting fast now, and I was glad to get some sunshine back in our lives. We spent Thanksgiving with Cathy, Christmas with Ali and Maggie, and New Year's Eve; I stayed home with my girls drinking hot chocolate with marshmallows. We tooted some noise makers, and after they had gone to bed, I watched the ball drop on television by myself. Jesse called and asked if I wanted to join him uptown for the New Year's Eve dance at the local bar and grill, but I told him I was staying home with the girls. He tried to get me to change my mind and get a babysitter, but I refused. Jesse gave up calling and leaving messages after that, and I missed him terribly but kept telling myself that it was for the best.

It was a long winter, and I was tired of shoveling snow and chopping ice off the sidewalks. We made the best of things, though. I taught the girls how to make a snowman, and they had a ball. We went sliding down Summit Hill on inner tubes, and I brought my movie camera along and captured the girls giggling all the way down the hill. They loved the outdoors. Cathy and I hung out a lot, and she was great with the girls and was a good friend. I could talk to her about everything, well, almost everything.

She often tried to convince me to go out with the guys she suggested, but I cut her off before she could talk too much about it.

She would stop, knowing that she wasn't getting anywhere. Then she would bring up Jesse, but I would instantly put my hand up to stop her. "Ugh, you're so stubborn," she laughed as we finished the dishes one evening that she had come over for dinner. After putting the kids down to bed that night, Cathy ran out to her car and brought in a 12-pack of beer, and announced that "Mommy time is over; ladies' night now begins." She giggled at her announcement, and I shook my head at her, "You are naughty," I teased.

We settled in the living room, I put in a movie for us to watch, and she cracked open two beers. It was nice to finally relax. The day was long, and I was tired. Suddenly the doorbell rang, and I looked at Cathy with eyebrows raised. She smiled that evil little grin of hers. "I will get it!" She jumped to her feet and ran to the door. "Who did you invite over, you little shit" I scolded. She just giggled and swung the door open. Two guys came in, and she pointed them to the kitchen to grab a beer out of the frig. I saw that it was Matt and Joey. Two guys that worked at the body shop uptown.

"Hey, Kally, how are you?" Joey asked as he took a swig out of his beer. He was tall and lean with brown wavy hair and blue eyes. Joey was one of those all-around nice guys that could talk your ear off if you let him, but he had a lot of interesting stories to tell. He was handsome and always wore a hat, and I often wondered if he was bald underneath that cap or what the deal was, but that night I found out. He wasn't bald. He was very flirtatious, though, and I felt a little uncomfortable when he plopped down next to me on the couch a little too close. I tried to scoot over, but he scooted right with me. Halfway through the movie, I had no idea what was happening because they were all chatting right through it, but we laughed and joked. I had forgotten what it was like to have a few beers and sit around with friends just hanging out. It was nice.

Since Cathy had gone through a divorce, she was a little friendly with Matt, which made Joey think that he had to be a little closer to me, but I made sure that I put a stop to that. "Cake, anyone" I jumped to my feet, trying to break free of Joey's wandering hands. "Cake? Now?" Cathy asked, looking a little frustrated with me. I just smiled and ran to the kitchen. Well, that didn't seem to work because Joey was right behind me, "I will help you, Kally," he announced. That left Cathy and Matt free to make out in my living room, and I was alone with Joey in my kitchen.

He was incredibly attractive, and I am a woman with hormones, and it had been so long since another man touched me. I didn't trust myself alone with him, and I surely didn't trust him alone with me, either. I shoved a plate of cake toward him, and he took the plate with one hand and grabbed my hand with his other, and pulled me closer to him. "Joey, I ...." He stopped me by pressing his fingers to my lips, "Shhhh," he quieted me and pulled me in for a long, enthusiastic kiss. My body gave in to him at once like putty in his hands.

When I tried to pull away, he only tugged me closer, pushing his body into mine and sending my body into a thrilling state of pleasure. His lips against my neck excited me in every way, and it felt so good to have a man hold me again, but I knew where this was all leading, and I knew I had to stop it, but my body longed for more. Suddenly I came to my senses when I heard Jenni screaming from her bedroom down the hall. I pushed Joey away from me and quickly straightened my blouse, and ran to check on Jenni, leaving Joey in the kitchen protesting. I comforted my daughter, that had woken up from a bad dream, and when I finally got her back to sleep, I came back out to the living room to find that Joey and Matt had left, and Cathy was lying on the couch fast asleep.

I was relieved that Jenni had woke up and put a stop to my moment of weakness and Joey and I hadn't gone any further, but I kept thinking that it was very nice to have a man's arms around me again and to feel those feelings of intimacy again that I thought I was incapable of feeling anymore. A simple touch can instantly arouse your body when a person feels lonely and hasn't been touched in quite some time. I sat in the armchair and picked up the phone, suddenly missing Jesse. I hadn't seen him or heard from him since New Year's Eve.

I glanced at the clock, which now read 1 am, picked up the phone, and dialed Jesse's number. I listened as the phone rang and rang. I was just about to hang up when Jesse answered with a scratchy, hoarse voice. "Hello," he said in almost a whisper. "I woke you up; I am so sorry," I lied, thrilled to hear his voice. "Kally? Are you okay?" He sounded worried and tired. "I am okay, Jesse; I just needed to talk to you," I told him with liquid courage running through my veins. "What's wrong, honey?" He continued, "You sound like you are sad." He was still worried. "I am coming over," he told me and hung up before I had the chance to tell him that it wasn't necessary.

Within minutes he was knocking on my front door. I opened the door and practically fell into his arms. He held me as I cried and told him how much I missed him and how lonely I had been without having him to talk to. He just kept holding me and petting the top of my head like a lost puppy. Then he took my chin and tilted my head up to look at him, and without a word, his mouth came down hard on mine.

I suddenly pulled away from him, and all the guilt came rushing back. Here I was just a couple of hours ago in the kitchen with Joey, ready to give myself to him, and now I was in Jesse's arms, eager to give myself to him. How could I be so cold? What kind of a person was I to betray my husband for one night of pleasure because I was so weak and lonely? I thought to myself. "I am sorry, Jesse, I can't," I told him with tears in my eyes. "Kally, you are killing me!" Jesse's face looked hurt and angry again, and he turned to leave. I grabbed his arm, and he brushed me away and slammed the door as he left.

I wanted to grab the door handle and fling it open and run after him and tell him I don't know what I am supposed to do or what I am supposed to feel; I have all these feelings inside of me, and then guilt rushes in for feeling this way. I get all confused and sad inside. I wanted to tell him I was sorry for putting him through all of this, but I just stood there and listened to his truck speed out of my driveway and said nothing. The tears fell down my cheeks, and I wondered if I would ever be happy again.

CHAPTER EIGHT

LEARNING TO FORGET

A couple of months later, when I was at work, I heard that Jesse's ex-wife had moved to Colorado with the kids, and Jesse packed up and moved right along with them. I could see that about him. He wouldn't want his kids to be so far away from him and would have done anything to be by their side. He had taken a job out there, put his house up for sale, and Jesse was gone, just like that. No goodbye, nothing. I had no right to be angry about it. The way I treated him, I really didn't deserve any explanations or goodbyes from him, but I was angry, or hurt was a better word, I guess.

Well, it was for the best, I kept telling myself. Now I could get back to focusing on raising my daughters and making a life for us without any distractions from Jesse. I secretly wished him the best and tried to put him out of my mind, which was no easy task. We had become close friends, but when he wanted to become more than that, I kept pushing him away until he finally decided to cut all ties. I just wished I had the chance to tell him goodbye.

Summer came, and Cathy kept trying to get me out of the house and out of my yard. I worked in the yard in my spare time, planting flowers and growing vegetables in my garden. My yard was amazing that summer. I had yellow and purple tulips planted all on the north side of the house. I dug a round corner of the yard, put down edging and rock, and planted all kinds of beautiful foliage and flowers. I made a little waterfall with a raised rock bed above. It was absolutely gorgeous.

The girls helped as much as they could, but mostly they played on the playground I had put in the yard for them. I bought a jungle gym and a teeter-totter for them to play on, and I filled the sandbox, which really made a mess, as they tracked it through the house every time they had to use the bathroom.

They were happy kids, though; this was the last summer we had before Carrie started school in the fall when she turned 6. I was going to start her in kindergarten the year before, but I felt she was too young. I planned a trip to see their gramma Ali and Auntie Maggie, which they were very excited about. I had the car packed and ready to roll on a Friday morning, and I had taken a week off from work. We started our trip, and Ali knew we were coming, so she made the girls a cherry pie and an apple pie for their arrival. We pulled up in front of her house, and Ali was sitting in her favorite spot on the porch in her swing.

I don't remember her looking so old and weak. My heart was immediately saddened for waiting so long to come and visit her, especially since I promised to visit often. It had been since Christmas that I had seen them. I ran to her with the girls right beside me and wrapped my arms around her in a big hug with tears in my eyes. "Kally, those girls have grown so big," she cried. She hugged them up and pinched their little cheeks as they giggled.

"Mike would be so proud of them," her voice trailed off with tears in her eyes. She missed him as much as I did, I thought to myself. I hugged her again. "I miss him too, every day, every moment," I whispered and began to cry. "What's wrong, Mommy?" Carrie said, tugging at my pant leg. I snapped out of it, turned to her, and hugged her tightly, "Nothing honey, mommy is just so happy to see your gramma, that's all," I lied, not wanting her to know that I was really missing her daddy.

Maggie came over that evening, and we all had a nice supper that Ali had cooked up. She made us her famous fried chicken and garlic mashed potatoes with sweet corn. I ate too much and was extremely tired after such a big meal. Ali told me to go and lie down for a while. She would watch the girls. I decided to take her up on her offer and went to our room to nap.

My body was like a limp rag doll, and I fell asleep as soon as my head hit the pillow. I awoke to the girls giggling coming from the kitchen. I went downstairs to see that they were all making cookies, and Ali was letting the girls help. Jenni had flour in her hair and all over her clothes, and Carrie was equally a mess, but I stood in the doorway smiling at how much fun they were all having together. "Well, it sure smells good around here," I told them. "Mommy, Mommy, we made you cookies" Jenni stood there beaming from ear to ear, holding a cookie out for me. I took it and bit into it with a big smile, showing her how happy and yummy it was.

I began rubbing my belly, telling her, "Yum, the best cookie I ever had." She was pleased. Looking at her big smile, I couldn't believe she was already 3 1/2 years old. Time had just whipped by so quickly. The week went by fast, and soon it was time to get back home and back to work. We said our goodbyes and gave our hugs, and we were in the car and back on the road towards home.

When we pulled back into our driveway, it was getting late, and both girls were fast asleep. I carried them in the house one at a time, put them down on the couch, and covered them up. Exhausted, I fell into the chair next to them and went to sleep without unpacking the car. We all slept in the living room that night, too lazy and tired to do the bedtime ritual, and didn't have the heart to wake them up. I was glad I chose to come home on Saturday, so I had all day Sunday to put things away and get Carrie ready for her first day of school on Monday.

I woke up early, and the girls were still sleeping on the couch. I went to check the mail, and it was plump full. I had asked Cathy to check it while I was gone, but apparently, she had forgotten. I pulled a letter out, and my heart skipped a beat as I read the front of the envelope. It was from Jesse. I stood there shaking, unable to open it for quite some time. Finally, I tore into it, and it read,

'Dear Kally, I hope everything is going okay for you and that one day you will be able to heal your heart and let people care for you the way you deserve to be cared for. I fell for you the day I saw you, and I think you also felt a connection to me, which is what scares you the most. I was upset the last time I saw you, and I am sorry I stormed off the way I did. I understand that you are scared to let people in, and I know that you feel you are betraying the vows that you made to Mike, but one day your heart will open again, and

I hope you will give me a call. Take care, sweet girl; I will miss you and hope to hear from you again one day. All my love, Jesse

I stood there, unable to move and stop the tears from flowing. I called Cathy, and she came over immediately. When she finished reading the letter, there were tears in her eyes. "Oh my God, Kally, you have to go to him." She told me. "I can't just run out to Colorado and uproot the lives that we made here" I shook my head. Jesse was right about one thing: I had a deep connection with him and missed him so much, but I was not going to move out to Colorado on a wild goose chase after the man. I had two daughters to think of, and we had made a life here. I put the letter in a box and tucked it under my bed. I decided to put the letter out of my mind and forget that I had even opened it, but it was no use; Jesse was on my mind as always.

I wanted to write back to him, but I couldn't tell him I missed him so much it hurt. I couldn't tell him that my heart was filled with love for him, and I dreamt about him most nights. I had to put it out of my mind and ignore his letter, or I knew that he would come back here immediately, and then he would resent me for being so far away from his children. I was not going to be in that position. I was not going to have his kids hate me for it either, so I tucked the letter away, and I lived with the hurt of not seeing him and possibly never hearing from him again. I was right. Years went by, and I didn't hear from Jesse.

I had heard he met a girl a couple of years back, and I think he married her. I had no right to be angry about that or sad. I tried to call his number once, in a moment of weakness and loneliness, but it was no longer in service. I don't know why I even bothered to try; I mean, after all, I had no right to interfere in his life.

CHAPTER NINE

TEN YEARS LATER

Sam had a heart attack the winter when my oldest daughter turned 16, and I became the newspaper's chief editor. The funeral was the most prominent funeral I had ever attended. Ella looked so distraught and old while her son, Brody, sat beside her, comforting her. She didn't want anything to do with the paper, but she couldn't bring herself to sell out either, and Brody was not interested in taking it over, so she asked me if I would run the whole show there, and I agreed. I told her that I wouldn't let her down, and I didn't.

Joey had been trying to get me to go out with him for years, and I refused to be involved with anything but work and the kids, but one day at the café shop eating lunch, he plopped into the booth next to me and asked me one more time. "Go out with me, Kally, to a movie this weekend? Dinner and a movie? That is all I ask." He had a pouty, teasing look on his face. "Okay," I replied to my surprise, and he jumped to his feet and hollered, "She said yes!" Everyone in the place started clapping their hands, and I blushed and laughed.

That Saturday, we went out to dinner and a movie. I enjoyed myself a lot, to my surprise. Joey was hilarious and did most of the talking, so I just listened and laughed a lot. We started dating more often then and became closer. He was handsome and funny and put my mind in a better place. I guess the whole town knew how much Joey liked me and how long he had waited for me to finally give him a date because, for weeks to come, all I heard from anyone was, "It's about time you gave that boy a chance." I started spending a lot of time with Joey, and the girls also liked him. The only downfall was Joey drank a lot, and that worried me. I didn't want to have a heavy drinker in my life and sometimes wondered if he had a problem with alcohol. That worried me a bit, but I brushed it off because it felt good to have a man hold me again.

The girls were so busy with school and sports. Jenni was in basketball, tall like her daddy was, and she looked a lot like Mike. She had his beautiful brown eyes. Carrie was a cheerleader for Wrestling, and she was more outspoken, whereas Jenni was quieter and had her head more into books than boys, like her sister. Carrie had her eye on the captain of the football team. I wouldn't say I liked that he was older than her by two years, and many other girls were also interested in him. He seemed to me like he was a player of many young, innocent girl's hearts, and I would be damned if he was going to be the one to win my daughter's heart. I kept close tabs on Carrie. She was headstrong, a lot like I was when I was young, and I did not want her to make bad choices as I had as a teenager.

"You can't protect her from everything, Kally," Cathy told me one day when we were having lunch at the café. "I know," I snapped, not meaning to sound so snotty. Cathy held her hand up, "Hey, I am on your side; I am just saying that Carrie is 16 years old, and the more you try to hold her back, the more she is going to want to run away," I nodded and apologized for being so cranky.

That evening Carrie ran downstairs and hollered, "Be home by 11," and out the door she went before I could chase her down to ask her where she was going. I was sitting on the couch at 11 pm, upset with her for leaving without asking, and ready to rip into her when she walked through the door, but she never showed up. At midnight I was worried and pacing the floor. I called Cathy, and she came over. "Calm down, Kally; she is a typical teenager who does not know how to tell time. She will come through that door any minute," Cathy scolded me for worrying so much. "I don't like it, Cathy. I have this ache inside that something is wrong". I told her worriedly.

When the phone rang, I ran to get it, "CARRIE?" I screamed out. "Kally, what's wrong?" Oh my God, it was Jesse. I started crying like a baby, "Oh God, Jesse Carrie is not home yet, and I know something has happened to her, and I don't know where to look or what to think or do...." "Stop, Kally, it's going to be okay," he reassured me. "I wish I could be there to help you look." He said.

"Are you okay, honey?" Jesse asked. Suddenly, I was angry. "Why are you calling me? You have not bothered to keep in touch with me for ten years now, and suddenly out of the blue, you call me up to see how I am doing and act like you care if I am, okay?" I yelled at him.

"It was just too hard, and when you didn't answer my letter, I assumed you didn't want to hear from me." His voice was sad on the phone, but I was not going to let my heart in again. "I'm sorry, Jesse, it was a long time ago, and I have no right to be upset with you. I am just upset with worry about Carrie." I told him. I had been hoping that Jesse would call me for years, and then I started yelling at him on the phone. What was wrong with me, I thought. Cathy was standing there staring at me with a smile, waiting to hear more of our conversation.

"I have to find Carrie now; Can I talk to you later?" I asked him. He agreed and told me to call him when I found her to let him know she was safe, and I focused back on my missing daughter. At 3 am, Carrie finally walked through the door, a drunken mess! A boy was holding her up and helping her in the house. The captain of the football team, none other! I gasped and lunged toward him, pushing him backward and grabbing my daughter before she could hit the floor. "I found her this way, Maam, and I brought her home before some other not-so-nice guys had their way with her." He snapped at me in his defense.

I looked him in the eyes and glared at him but softened when I knew he was telling the truth. "Thank you, Josh, I am sorry for assuming, and you, young lady, we will talk in the morning." Josh helped me get Carrie upstairs and into bed, but she lunged out of bed in an instant, and Josh grabbed her arm and helped her to the bathroom to unload her alcohol level. I stood at the door and watched as Josh gently held my daughter's hair back for her and rubbed her back while she hurled and heaved, and I thought, "Wow, did I misjudge this boy?" He was one of the sweetest teen boys I had met.

I went downstairs to Cathy and told her goodnight and that I would talk to her tomorrow. She tried to bring up the subject of

Jesse again, but I put my hand up in protest and gently nudged her to the door. The following day, I dialed Jesse's number on my caller ID, and when he answered, I told him that Carrie was home safely. I told him about her condition that she came home in and how angry I was, but I was so glad that she was safe at home. We talked for over an hour, and he told me that he was still working out in Colorado doing heating and air-conditioning; his girls were doing well.

Jesse told me he met someone and got married, but he told me that it was a mistake and wasn't happy. He told me he was planning a trip home soon, and it would be nice to see me and catch up. I told him I was seeing someone, and that might not be a good idea, but he just brushed it off and said, "Kally, we are friends, and we will always have that! "See you soon, sweetheart," he said and hung up the phone before I could say another word.

The next day Joey stopped in at the newspaper while I was working, and he leaned in to kiss me and set a small box on my desk. "For you, my love," it read on the top of the box. My heart sank, and I wanted to run away instantly. I knew what was in that box, and I just couldn't open it for fear of hurting him when I had to tell him no. We had been dating for a year, and I wasn't sure I was ready for this or if I ever wanted this again, but he didn't give me a chance to open it.

He was down on one knee and grabbed the box, and opened it up to me, "Marry me, Kally, and I will make you the happiest woman on this earth; I promise you that, babe" I looked at his sweet face waiting for my reply and with tears in my eyes I didn't have the heart to tell him no so I reached out and touched his cheek and told him I would think about it. Not the answer he wanted to hear, but at least it was not a no.

He grabbed me up in his arms and kissed me, yelling, "Whoo hoo!" The office members cheered and clapped as if I had said yes. "I will pick you up at eight tonight, wear something nice," he ordered, and out the door, he flew. I am sure to tell the whole town that I had said yes. I tried to stop him, but he ignored my protests. I looked at the girls in the office smiling at me and yelled, "I didn't say yes. I said I would think about it." They just laughed. I rolled my eyes and got back to work.

That night I wore a black dress with an open back and my black and silver high heels, with a silver shawl around my shoulders, "Wow, Mom, you look hot," Carrie whistled. I blushed and turned to smack her in the arm playfully. Jenni chuckled. I sat the girls down and told them that Joey had asked me to marry him, and they screamed with delight. "So, you're both happy about that?" I asked.

The girls approved, the town agreed, and it was nice lying next to someone again, and the sex was good, too, when he was sober. He would make me happy I kept trying to convince myself, but something just wasn't there. I did not feel passionate and excited. I told the girls I would think about it and that I hadn't told Joey yes. "I am not sure this is what I want," I told Carrie and Jenni as they sat on my bed, watching me give my hair a final touch-up. Jenni walked over to me and said, "Mom, Daddy would want you to be happy, but if Joey doesn't make you feel happy, then say no" She was such a wise girl for her age. I talked to the girls about their daddy quite often, and we went through pictures too. I wanted to ensure that both girls knew what a wonderful man Mike was and how much he loved his girls.

Joey picked me up right on time. I gave the girls a quick hug as I walked out the door and went to dinner. He wanted to set a date and tried to convince me that we should get married in August, but he ignored that I had told him I would think about it. "Stop, Joey, I didn't agree to get married; I am not sure I am ready for all of this" I watched as his eyes lost the spark, and he finally got what I was saying. Joey brought me home around 11 pm, and I invited him to stay the night. We made love that night, and he held me in his arms afterward. I lay there with my backside cuddled against his naked body, and I felt content but not truly happy. I lay there as Joey fell asleep and thought about Jesse's phone call.

I wondered why he was calling me after ten years, and if he wasn't happy in his marriage, was he planning on getting a divorce? I wondered why I hadn't asked more questions when I talked to him. Thinking about him made my insides smile again, and I realized how much I had missed him over the years and how often I wondered how he was doing. I fell asleep thinking about him and what I would say to him, if and when, I would see him again. I decided that I would call him again in the morning.

Morning Came, and I quickly ran downstairs to start breakfast before anyone else got up. I made a pot of coffee first and decided to call Jesse while the house was still quiet. "Hello," his sleepy voice was on the line. "I'm sorry I woke you," I told him. "Kally, I'm glad you called back." He asked about Carrie, and I told him she was still very grounded. He laughed. "I'm sure she won't try that again." He said. Jesse told me that he would like to get together soon and catch up. He told me that he would be in town in a few days to visit his sister and would like to see me. "You have been in town a few times in the last ten years to visit her; why all of a sudden, this time, you want to see me?" I asked.

Cathy had told me every time Jesse was in town, and I made sure that I stayed close to home during those times so that I would never accidentally run into him. "I just need to see you, Kally, and talk with you." He sounded so sad. "I'm not sure that is a good idea, Jesse, I have been seeing Joey, and I am not sure he would like that," I told him. Jesse pleaded with me to see him just once, and I reluctantly agreed. He told me he would be in town this Friday and would call me to make plans. I heard someone awake in the house then, and I quickly said I had to go and hung up the phone.

That morning after breakfast and everyone had left to start their day, I called Cathy and asked her to come for coffee. I told her about my conversation with Jesse. "Oh wow, Kally, what are you going to do?" She said with a smile that told me she loved to be a part of some big secret. "Joey has been a part of my life and the girls' lives for quite some time. He has been there for the girls and me, but I don't feel like I am in love with him," I told her with disappointment in my voice. Cathy told me that if I didn't feel passion for Joey after all these years, it wouldn't ever be there and that I should end things with him now. "Either way, he is going to be hurt, Kally, you can't avoid that, but if you're not in love with Joey, you need to be honest with him." "I know, but he is so good to the girls and ...." Cathy held up her hands and cut me off.

"You can't marry him because everyone else thinks he is right for you, Kally," Cathy said. "I know, but why can't things just continue the way they are without getting married?" I said, already knowing the answer. I knew that it was not fair to Joey and that he wanted to be married and be a part of our family and move in together, but I just wanted things to stay the same and live my own life but have him there when I needed him. You could say I was using him so that he could take away some of the loneliness I felt in my life, and I knew that things were bound to change when he started wanting more from me.

That night Joey came over, and the girls were out with friends, so I took the opportunity to talk seriously with Joey. I made supper that evening and started the conversation I had been avoiding for years. "Joey, we need to talk about our relationship," I told him. He ignored my words and changed the subject to something that had happened at work. I think he knew what I was about to say he wasn't going to like, and so by avoiding the conversation, he could make it go away. "Joey, stop," I demanded and continued what I needed to say.

"We have had this relationship that has been good up until now when you want things to move forward, and I can honestly say that I do not want to get married. I don't feel that way about you, and it isn't fair to you if I let this continue the way it is." I raised one hand to him when he tried to interrupt me and complain.

"Let's be honest, Joey, you know that we have been good friends for years now, but I have treated you more like a friend than a partner in this relationship. I know you want more from me, and I just can't give you what you want," I said. Joey rolled his eyes and tried to argue and convince me that we were good together until I became frustrated and blurted it out. "I don't love you, Joey" I looked him in the eyes, and it killed me to see the pain in them.

"I know you don't, Kally, but I can take care of you, and I love you; you will grow to love me, and we will be good together" I stopped him, and I reached out and touched his arm, "Joey, I need to feel the passion in my life with whomever I end up with, I need to feel love in my heart, and I don't feel that way with you. We don't make love; we have sex. It isn't fair to you that I can't give you what you deserve." I explained. " I need to end this before it goes any further, and I hurt you even more," I announced.

I told him I needed to be alone now, and he needed to go home. I told him I didn't want to see him anymore, and it was over. He got up from his chair, leaned towards me and kissed me gently on the top of my head, and with tears in his eyes, said goodbye. It was hard to see him like that when we had become such good friends over the years, but I knew how my heart felt when I was truly in love, and I knew that I had never felt that way with Joey. I also called Jesse that day and told him that I wasn't going to meet him when he was in town and that it was best that we stayed away from each other.

I never told Jesse that I broke it off with Joey because I knew he would have come over when he was in town. I was back to holding my heart hostage again and cooping myself up at home and work. I just put it in my head that Mike was the one chance I had at love, and he was gone, so I didn't have the right to be happy again until I met him again in another life.

That Friday, I stayed home from work and kept busy around the house. I wanted to make sure that I didn't run into Jesse in town if he truly was going to be home that weekend. Well, that didn't help because Friday evening he called me. I didn't answer the phone, but Jesse was at my front door knocking within the hour. I could pretend that I wasn't home, but my car was in the driveway, and he would just keep knocking, so I went to answer the door. Our eyes met, and he instantly swept me up in a bear hug, and it felt good. When he put me down, he began telling me how much he missed me and how often he thought of me over the years.

Something drew me to this man even after so many years had passed. It angered me when I thought, how could he have been thinking about me and missing me if he didn't even bother getting in touch with me for ten years? When I looked into his eyes, my heart pounded faster again, my cheeks felt flushed, and the same old feelings returned again.

He came in, and we sat at the kitchen table talking about the kids, the lifetime events over ten years, his sister, Ali, and Maggie, and how much we missed talking to each other. It was like no time at all had passed by. I told him about Joey, and I's relationship and that he had asked me to marry him, but it never felt right. I told him I didn't want him to leave again, but I knew he was going to.

"I have to go back until the kids graduate," he told me. "I don't plan on staying in Colorado, Kally, but I do have to stay for a while longer," he said sadly. Jessica was 16 years old and had a couple more years of high school, and Bella was 14. That was another four years before he planned on moving back, and a lot can change in four years, I thought to myself.

After a couple of hours of visiting, he stood up to say goodbye again. Jesse hugged me close, and my body trembled. His lips softly brushed against my neck, and he kissed my neck, then stood back and made eye contact, grabbed me up, and kissed me passionately.

All those feelings of passion and excitement flooded my whole body. I gently pushed Jesse back and told him goodbye. "I promise to stay in touch this time, Kal," he told me, and I nodded as he walked out the door, got in his truck, and drove away. I never told the girls Jesse had stopped by, but I mistakenly told Cathy. She was so excited that she couldn't stop asking questions. I told her it was just a visit and it was good to see him. She didn't believe me, but she got the hint that I no longer wanted to discuss it.

CHAPTER TEN

SAYING GOODBYE

Before I knew it, three years had flown by, and Carrie was graduating from high school. I could not believe how quickly the years went by; my children have grown up already. I planned a party for her and invited Ali and Maggie to come and spend the weekend. Joey and I were still seeing each other off and on. I guess he decided that it was okay that I did not want to marry him as long as we still could be together. I decided I would rather have Joey around than be lonely and alone.

The big day was here, and we were getting ready for the commencement ceremony. I decorated the house, had sloppy Jo's, potato salad, chips, and salsa, and made a couple of salads for the party. I had the bakery in town make a huge cake with a baby picture and her graduation picture, and it read, "Congratulations, Carrie, on your Graduation Day ." she looked beautiful in her gown, with her brown wavy hair all curled up in locks flowing down her shoulders. I made sure I snapped many pictures that day, and when we all returned to the house to celebrate, I walked in the door to see the answering machine flashing.

I listened to the message, and it was from Maggie. She told me they would not attend the ceremony or the party because Ali had a heart attack and was in the hospital. Tears welled up in my eyes as I listened to Maggie's words. I was looking for them at the ceremony and wondered why they didn't attend, and I was worried, but I didn't think anything like this happened. "The attack was bad, and the doctors are not hopeful that she will pull through." She stated in her message. I picked up the phone and called Maggie to see how she was doing.

Maggie sounded different on the phone. Tired and scared, I guess. "I should come out there to be with you," I told her. "No, Kally, this is your daughter's day, and there really is nothing you can do, so please just celebrate your daughter's achievement" I reluctantly agreed and told her to keep me posted on any changes, and we hung up the phone. I pulled myself together and decided it was best not to say anything to the girls on this day. I didn't want to ruin this day for Carrie and make her day so sad.

I got through the evening and started cleaning up when the last people left. Carrie had gone out with friends to the graduation parties, and she let Jenni tag along too, so it was just me at home. I looked around the quiet house, and suddenly tears filled my eyes. Soon Jenni would graduate, and I would be left all alone with no one to share my life with, I thought to myself, and the aching in my heart got worse. I kept thinking about Ali, too, and worried about how she was doing. I called Maggie to see how things were going, and there was no answer, so I left a message for her to call me back with any news, no matter what time it was.

The next morning came, and no word from Maggie, so I called again, and finally, after about six rings, I heard her tired and worried voice on the phone. "How is Ali?" I asked her. "There is no change, she is weak, and it is only a matter of time, Kally," she started to cry on the phone. "I will pack a few things and come out to stay with you for a few days if that's okay?" I asked her. "I really need this too, so please don't say no, Maggie," I told her, and she agreed. I hung up the phone and called Carrie and Jenni to let them know. They had stayed overnight at a friend's house after the graduation party so that no one would be drinking and driving. I told Carrie my plans and told her what was going on. She was worried but told me to call as soon as I arrived so that she would know I was okay.

I was packed and ready to go by 2 pm. I stopped at the gas station to fill my car with gas when a familiar voice rang out behind me. "Hey, sexy lady," it was Jesse. I knew before I even turned around to see. I stood there for a while before I turned to look at him. He placed his hand on my shoulder, and I spun around quickly then. "Hey, when did you get to town?" I asked, trying to act calmly as if his presence still didn't excite me. He didn't let me act that way for long; he just grabbed me and hugged me tightly, "God did I miss you, honey," he told me, not letting me pull away when I tried.

Jesse noticed the suitcase in the car and asked where I was going. I told him about Ali, and he immediately wanted to go with me. "Let me drive you there, Kally; you are upset" "No ."I quickly responded. I told him it wasn't a good idea, but he demanded I let him drive me to Ali and Maggie's. "I don't want you to come with me, Jesse" I held my ground and firmly told him no. I told him goodbye, ran to pay for my gas, and drove off. My phone rang, and it was him, but I ignored it, and he tried three times again, but I didn't pick it up. I thought to myself, he has a lot of nerve, he is married, and now he wants to come into my life again and make my heart hurt again. No, I had to put him out of my mind for good. He was not my friend or anything to me, for that matter. I did not owe him anything.

I had a pleasant visit with Maggie, and Ali showed signs of improvement, but it was unfortunate when Maggie had to decide to put Ali into the nursing home. She could no longer care for herself and needed a nursing staff around her from now on. It broke Maggie's heart to sell the house and start selling Ali's things to pay the nursing home bills. I tried to help her through it the best that I could. I promised I would visit her more often, and we needed to stay close, and she agreed. She told me that she would take some time off work to see us.

She missed the girls a lot and wanted to be there for Jenni's graduation. I told her it was understandable that she missed Carrie's graduation, but she still felt terrible about it and gave me a card to give her from Ali and her. I arrived home and immediately felt the loneliness creep back into my life again when the girls led such busy lives, and I was home alone much of the time. I decided I needed to start a hobby, so I enrolled in another photography class and dug out my old cameras.

This class was held at the community center and was a six-week session. I toyed around with photography a lot when I was a kid, and I took many pictures for the newspaper, but I have always loved photography, so I started taking pictures of wildflowers and wilderness scenery. It kept my mind busy, but my heart was still lonely.

At the end of July, I went to the grocery store to pick up some milk and bread. I was at the checkout when I heard someone talking about Jesse. My ears automatically leaned in closer, and I looked over to see that it was Jesse's ex-wife Laurie and another lady I didn't know. "What was she doing back in town," I thought to myself. I heard her say Jesse was back too, and my heart started beating faster. I dropped my purse to the floor when I fumbled for my checkbook. They both looked my way then, and I smiled foolishly because they obviously caught me eavesdropping.

"Clumsy, I guess," and shrugged my shoulders. "You are Kally, right?" Laurie said. "Yes, that's me" I smiled again, looking rather stupid, I thought. "Have you talked to Jesse yet? He is back in town, you know?" She gave me a smirk that made me question what she was thinking. "No, I haven't talked to him in quite some time; how is he?" I asked, trying not to sound too interested. "He is doing good now that he is back. He hated it out in Colorado, and that wife of his really took him for a ride" I raised one eyebrow to find out the dirt, but she just walked away, telling me that it was nice to see me.

Did that mean he is not with his wife anymore? Did it mean she left him? What did it all mean, I wondered. I started to wonder if I should call him, but I immediately shook that out of my mind, but of course, he was back on my mind again. Well, I didn't have to wonder long because as I was coming out of the post office, I was fumbling for my car keys in my purse and ran smack into him as I opened the door. "Sorry," I looked up to see him staring at me. My heartbeat instantly was faster, and the palms of my hands were sweaty.

"Kally? How are you?" he asked, grabbing my hand. I pulled it away quickly. "Fine, Jesse, how are you?" I asked, trying not to sound so excited to see him. "I have been meaning to call you and let you know that I moved back," he said. "Oh, well, I heard you were back, small town and all," I replied coldly. Jesse grabbed my hand then and tugged me out the door towards his truck. "What are you doing?" I demanded with a whine. "We need to talk! You were my friend Kally, and now you hate me, and I need to know why?" He kept tugging me to his truck and opened the door. "Please get in," he demanded in a friendly but firm way.

"Fine, whatever," I sounded irritated. Is that what he thought? That I hated him? How could he believe that? Doesn't he know that when he touches me, my heart melts? Can't he hear my heart pounding when he is next to me? I wondered.

Jesse drove out to the lake and picked a secluded place on a trail in the woods to park his truck. What was I doing in this truck? I thought, "Kally," Jesse's voice brought me back to the present. "What" I snapped. "I missed you so much, girl, don't you know that?" My face softened when he touched my arm, and I wanted to grab and kiss him, but I didn't. "I have to get back Jesse," I told him. He put his arm around me and pulled me closer to him, and tears rose in my eyes. I sank in next to him and started to cry.

"What is wrong, baby girl," he asked. I told him about Ali and how I needed to go out there and be with her. I told him she was now in a nursing home waiting to die, which broke my heart. In a way, I was telling him the truth because that is why I was emotional and sad, but I was also an emotional wreck because I was sitting next to a man that I fell in love with years ago, but I couldn't tell him that for fear that he would love me back and I would be happy, and then it would all disappear again, and my heart would break all over again.

We sat in his truck in silence for a long time, and Jesse just held me in his arms and let me cry until I was weak. "I really have to get back now," I told him. He started the truck and pulled out into the clearing. We drove back to town in silence, and I wondered what he was thinking but didn't ask. Jesse pulled up next to my car, and Cathy was coming out of the post office when we pulled up.

"Hey, you two, isn't this a blast from the past?" she smiled a curious and nosy smile at us both. "Cathy, don't read anything into this," I snapped. She just shrugged her shoulders with a grin, "Nice to see you again, Jesse; this town needs a little spice in it again," she teased. I snapped at her to shut up and jumped in my car, looking back at Jesse and giving him a wave goodbye. 'I'll call you," he yelled back, and I drove off, pretending not to hear him.

Since Joey and I were still seeing each other in a casual friendship-with-benefits relationship, I knew that he would disapprove of me seeing Jesse or talking to him. Joey still came over, and that night he was in the living room when the phone rang. It was Jesse, and I scurried out the back door to take the phone call. With a whisper, I said hello, and Jesse told me to meet him at Gullies on the corner. "No, I can't," I told him. "I will not be the talk of the town, Jesse, and I will not lie to Joey," I snapped. "So, tell Joey you're meeting an old friend for a beer at Gully's," he teased. "No," I snapped again. He just laughed. Just then, I heard Joey call out my name, and I told Jesse I had to go, "Don't call me Jesse," I demanded. He laughed again and told me that he would talk to me later.

"Plan your trip to see Ali and let me know when you are going," he told me as he hung up the phone, not waiting for my response. I ran back into the house, and Joey was standing in the kitchen. "Where were you?" he demanded. "I took the garbage out," I lied. "I know he is back in town, ya know," he said, not believing me. "Who?" I acted stupid. "Come on, Kally; you know damn well I am talking about Jesse. I know you talked to him today" he looked annoyed at me then. "Damn small towns," I thought. "Yes, I talked to Jesse today; he is doing fine," I told him, acting like it was no big deal. "What did the two of you talk about?" he pried further. "What is with the 20 questions" I snapped.

"Can't two old friends talk?" I grabbed a few dishes off the table and put them in the sink rather loudly. "Wow, you don't have to get so defensive," he hollered. "Better drop it then, Joey, unless you are trying to pick a fight," I warned him. I also reminded him that he and I were just friends with benefits, and there were no other strings attached to that. He dropped it then and walked back into the living room, mumbling. I hated when he mumbled. If you have something to say, then say it, but mumbling just to let the other person know you are upset but not wanting them to really hear what you are saying is a coward's way of fighting.

I went to bed that night upset, and Joey slept on the couch again. Joey and I did not live together, but he stayed over a lot. I sometimes think he stayed because he wanted to always keep his eyes on me. Joey was insecure in that way, and I didn't like that about him, but I guess I understood Joey's insecurities when it came to Jesse and knowing that I didn't carry the same feelings for Joey as he did for me.

Maybe he could see right through me and knew how I felt about Jesse; I don't know. I tried not to let it show. Deep down, I knew it wasn't very good of me to keep stringing Joey along the way I had. I know I was honest with him about my feelings, but I also knew that Joey had strong feelings for me and my girls, and I am sure it drove him crazy that I didn't love him back.

The following day, I told Joey that I was going to go and see Ali. He told me he would go with me, but he wouldn't take any more time off from work until our honeymoon. I rolled my eyes at him and said whatever. Joey knew we weren't getting married, but he kept pressing the issue daily. It was annoying. I said that was fine, not letting it show that I didn't really want him to come along anyway.

I told Jenni about my plans to see Ali, and she said she couldn't go along because of basketball practice, and she had a game coming up. Carrie was packing to move into her new apartment so that she could start school in the fall. Some of her friends were helping her move everything, and she would be all settled in her new apartment before I returned. I packed up a few things and was ready to leave by noon. I ran to the bank to get some cash, and I took the time to call Jesse and let him know I was going.

"Let me come with you, Kally," he asked. "It's not a good idea, Jesse," I told him, even though I wanted him by my side in the worst way. "Please, Kally, let me come with you," he said again, ignoring my first reply. "I don't know, Jesse; I have to run into the bank; I will call you back," I said. When I came out of the bank, Jesse was sitting in the front seat of my car. I jumped in the car, "What the hell are you doing, trying to get me into trouble?" I yelled.

"Just drive, Kally; I am coming with you" I shook my head, frustrated with him, but I drove off. I made sure I took the side streets out of town and not down the main street with eyes gawking at us. "Already, I feel like I am doing something wrong, Jesse," I said, feeling guilty.

Jesse touched my hand and told me it would be okay. "Two old friends need time to catch up," he smiled. I shook my head again and rolled my eyes at him. He just chuckled and squeezed my hand. I reached the end of town, and I became more relaxed. "This isn't right, Jesse," I said, feeling guilty again. "Kally, I know this trip will be hard on you, and I just want to be there to support you through it. Is there something wrong with that?" he caressed my hand, and I moved it away quickly, not wanting him to know that his touch thrilled me. I pulled over and let Jesse drive when he asked. I was tired and distracted, so it was probably safer that he drove.

I fell asleep for a while to the soft country music on the radio, and when I awoke, we were pulling up to Ali's house. I told Maggie that I was coming, and she was waiting for us to arrive. She opened the door and gave me a big hug. She glanced at Jesse, and I quickly introduced them, letting her know he was a good friend. She smiled and gave Jesse a second look as if she were sizing him up. "This is Jesse," I said as Maggie shook his hand. Jesse said how sorry he was about her mother's health. "She is not any better, Kally. I am glad you came to say goodbye," she told me. I gasped, unable to catch my breath, remembering how I felt when I got the news that Mike had died. I couldn't stop the tears from forming in my eyes.

Maggie seemed to be taking it well, though. We all drove to the hospital that evening, and when I walked into Ali's room and saw her hooked up to all those machines, the tears came again. It was me that could not stop crying. I didn't get to see Ali as much as I would have liked to, and now the girls were all grown up, and they didn't really know what a wonderful woman Ali was and how she took Mike in and raised him as her own when her daughter abandoned Mike.

Jesse slipped his arm around me, and I almost felt like Maggie would think I was cheating on Mike, so I pulled away from Jesse. "It's good that you have a friend to lean on," Maggie said as if she knew what I was thinking, and she was giving me her blessing. Ali was weak, but when she opened her eyes and looked at me, she smiled an old, soft, gentle smile. She tried to reach for my hand but could not lift it very far, so I went to her and held her hand.

In a whisper, she told me, "It's good to see you one last time. You are an angel that made my angel as happy as he could be for almost four years of his life. I will tell him that you miss him; and that you found someone to love you again. I am glad you finally found him. He will be happy to hear that." Her voice grew weaker, and I squeezed her hand gently, "I love you, Ali" She squeezed my hand slightly, and then she was gone with a smile on her face. I burst into tears, and Jesse grabbed me and held me tightly. Maggie stood there with tears in her eyes, and Jesse reached out his arms and hugged her too. "She is in a better place now, Kally," Maggie whispered and touched my cheek. I nodded, sobbed, and buried my face in Jesse's chest again.

We stayed and planned the funeral arrangements with Maggie for the next few days. The girls drove up for the funeral and arrived early that morning so they could help with anything we needed. Carrie was surprised to see Jesse standing there, and she shot me a look of confusion and raised her right eyebrow questioning me. I just grabbed her hand and told her we would talk later. "Come on, we have to get to the funeral home," I said as I lifted their suitcases and brought them into the guest room.

The funeral went quickly, and a lot of people were there showing their sympathy to Maggie. A lot of them hugged me as if they knew who I was, which confused me a little because I had no clue who they were, but I just got through the day the best that I could, and I thanked God that Jesse was there by my side to help me through it. "Ali told everyone she knew about you and the girls and how happy you made her boy," Maggie said with a smile. I smiled back and suddenly realized why everyone felt like they knew the girls and me.

After a few days, we hugged Maggie goodbye and told her to keep in touch and visit soon, and we headed for home, and the girls followed behind.

CHAPTER ELEVEN

TRAGIC MISTAKES

Carrie was going to stay the night before heading back to college in the morning. Her new apartment was off campus that she rented with another girl, and she had a part-time job as a receptionist at a Dental office until she started college in the fall. Jenni missed her terribly, but they talked on the phone all the time, and she enjoyed having the room to herself. When we pulled into town, I told Jesse that I had to run to the office to collect some paperwork I needed to get caught up.

I drove Jesse to his truck, called the girls, and told them I would be home shortly. At the office, I gathered up the things I needed, and as I was about to get back in my car, Jesse drove up and asked me to get in and go for a ride with him so we could talk. I climbed into his truck, and he drove off. Suddenly Jesse pulled off the road into a clearing in the woods and veered around a curve out of sight from town. "What are you doing" I shrieked in surprise. "We need to have some alone time, Kally; I have to talk to you ." He sounded eager.

We came to a stop, and he jumped out and ran around to my side of the truck, opened my door, and reached for my hand. I let him help me out of the truck, and he pulled me towards a little shack out in the woods. "Where are we? What is this place?" I demanded, sounding a little panicked. "Come on honey, it is only my hunting shack," he reassured me that I was safe. I always felt safe with Jesse; I wasn't worried about my safety, I was concerned because I knew what was going to happen, and I knew that I should have gone straight home. Still, I didn't, and now here I was alone with Jesse again, unsure I could stop myself from whatever was going to happen.

Jesse opened the door and pulled me in. There was a twin-sized bed in the corner with a plaid comforter neatly placed on it and a pillow with the same colors. There was green carpet and pine wood ceilings and walls. It smelled of pine trees inside as well. There was a small table and a couple of old chairs sitting at the table. I quickly sat down with my hands in my lap, nervous as a young schoolgirl and not saying a word. Jesse knelt to his knees in front of me and took my hands in his. He looked into my eyes and touched my cheek, wiping the hair that had fallen on my face like he had done many times before.

"Kally, you don't have to be nervous around me, you know that," he told me with a stern, calm voice. The tears came to my eyes before I could stop them, and he wrapped his arms around me and pulled me close to him. My body trembled as I melted into his arms for comfort and warmth. We both sunk to the floor together, and his hands searched every part of my body. His mouth came down on mine hard and full of so much passion that we had missed out on for so many years. I responded fiercely with pleasure as my body pressed against his, and I lost control completely.

I missed him more than words could say, and I didn't want this ever to end. Everything, everyone, was clear off my mind. The girls, Ali, Maggie, work, and yes, even Joey. I found love for the second time in my life and felt like this was where I truly belonged. I let my body feel every bit of warmth and love Jesse was offering me. His lips softly caressed my breasts as he opened my blouse and removed my clothing one piece at a time.

I reached up to him, pulled his shirt up over his head, and pulled him down on my bare skin, feeling his tanned, rugged body and soaking it up like it was the last bit of sunshine on earth. His mouth moved down my body, and there was no stopping, no thinking about stopping. I only wanted more of him. I pushed my body upwards, pressing my thighs against him and grabbing his hair. He suddenly grabbed me with one hand behind my back, and I squealed out in delight and pleasure as his tongue was inside me, sending my body into complete convulsions.

We held nothing back that day as we lay there rolling around that floor, giving each other the pleasure we had wanted for so many years and showing each other how much we missed each other and enjoyed one another. He rolled me over onto my belly and gently climbed on top of me, kissing my back and gliding his hands down my thighs. I felt him enter me, and again I screamed out in pleasure, and he shoved himself deeper inside of me, pulling me fiercely towards him closer like we were to be one person. After my body exploded with all the love I felt inside for him, I sunk to the carpet in exhaustion, and Jesse followed, lying on my back, caressing my skin softly. "I love you more than anything in this world, Kal," he whispered in my ear. I smiled and drifted off to sleep. I awoke to the sound of a gunshot and jumped up, startled. Jesse was lying next to me on the floor; both of us had nothing on except a sheet draped across our bodies. Jesse opened his eyes and pulled me closer to him, smiling. "Did you hear that gunshot" I shrieked.

"It's okay, Kally, it is hunting ground, ya know" he smiled again and pulled me back down next to him. I reluctantly placed my head on his chest and snuggled in next to him again, but suddenly snapped back to reality and sat up quickly again. "What time is it, Jesse? I have to get home. The girls are going to wonder, and, and... "my words drifted off, not wanting to say that Joey probably was waiting at my house wondering where I was.

Suddenly I felt guilty and awful. "Kally, we didn't do anything wrong, don't make this wrong," he said sternly. I nodded my head, not quite believing him that it wasn't wrong. After all, I was still seeing another man, and now I was lying naked next to the man I fell in love with long ago. "I have to go, Jesse," I told him, and he looked at me with sadness in his eyes and nodded.

"Don't turn this into something wrong, Kally; I beg of you," he said as he began to get dressed. I buttoned my blouse up and finished getting dressed. I patted my hair down to try and make it look like I wasn't rolling around the floor for hours, but it was useless. Everyone was going to know, I thought to myself. They would all take one look at me and see that I was unfaithful to Joey. Even though Joey and I were not in a relationship that was moving forward, I knew he would not want me to be with another man while I was seeing him. It was wrong of me to do such a thing.

Jesse looked at me with sadness in his eyes and shook his head, knowing that I had already had feelings of guilt inside of me and I had already turned our day into something wrong. He touched my cheek gently, "Come on honey, I will take you home"

The ride was silent and awkward, and when we came to the street where I had parked my car, Jesse jumped out and came to open my door. I slid out of his truck, not taking his hand to help me, and with tears in my eyes, I looked at him and didn't say a word. He touched my cheek again and wiped my tears away. "I love you, Kally. It is not wrong to be with someone that you love more than life," he told me, and he turned and jumped back in his truck and was gone, leaving me to stand there with tears running down my cheeks. I ran to my car sobbing and sat in the car for a while, trying to pull myself together before going home. When I walked in the front door, everyone was sitting in the living room, and they looked up at me when I entered the room.

Carrie shot me a disapproving look as she knew exactly where I was, and maybe that was just my imagination from all the guilt that I felt; I don't know, but it seemed like she was pretty, quiet all night with me. Joey was there too, and he didn't get up to hug me or ask me how I was or anything. He just sat there and continued to watch the football game on tv, glanced up, and said, "Oh, Hi, your home" I nodded, and that was it. I was glad that he didn't say more, though. I went to my room, unpacked my suitcases, and sorted the dirty clothes to start the laundry. Carrie knocked gently on my bedroom door then, and before I said to come in, she was already standing in the doorway. "Where were you, Mom?" she asked. I looked at her, and not wanting to lie to her, the tears in my eyes started again.

She rushed to my side and wrapped her arms around me. "Mom, what is wrong?" she demanded. I told her I was okay and just a little sad today. Not believing me, she looked at me with that eyebrow raised again, "You were with Jesse, weren't you? She already knew. I nodded my head, unable to stop the tears from forming quicker. She took both my hands in hers, squeezed them tightly, and looked me in the eyes, and I suddenly realized that my little girl was all grown up.

"Mom, you love Jesse! That is so obvious to so many people who know you two! You both have been fighting your feelings for so many years, but you always come back to each other and find some reason to walk away from each other again. You have hurt each other for so many years, not meaning to, but you both have broken hearts that only the two of you can mend. We all know that! When are the two of you going to figure that out?" she lectured me like I was the child and she was the parent.

I just listened to this suddenly adult-looking child of mine and realized she was right. I loved Jesse with all my heart, and for so many years, I thought it was wrong to love someone again after I had given my heart to Mike. I felt I was betraying him somehow, but Ali told me that Mike would be so happy that I found happiness again. Had Ali also given me her approval? I thought. Carrie touched my cheek and wiped away a tear lingering underneath my eye. "Be happy, Mom; we all want that for you," she said, and she turned and walked out of the room.

How did she get to be so bright? I thought. I smiled then and felt better for a while until that night when Joey came up to bed. I was in the bathroom brushing my teeth and pulled my nightshirt on to go to bed, and when I came out of the bathroom, Joey was lying in my bed. I jumped back, a bit startled. Joey turned to look at me and pulled back the cover, patting the sheet next to him for me to get into bed next to him.

"You are staying overnight?" I asked, suddenly acting as if he had never done this before. I had to snap out of this and act like nothing was wrong or nothing had changed. How could I do this? I thought. How can I jump into bed with Joey knowing what he wants right now when I was just with Jesse not more than 3 hours ago? I reached for my book on the end table. "I think I am going to read for a while," I told him. He grabbed my hand and pulled me, so I lost my balance and fell on top of him. He had his arms around me.

"Read? Not a chance, darling; I have not seen you in a week," he teased with his hands going up my shirt. I pushed him away and tried to get back up with him, holding me closer, and told him to stop. "The girls are home, and they will hear us," I told him, hoping that he would believe my reasoning. I wanted him to stop. He didn't listen to my words, and he suddenly rolled me over and was on top of me, kissing my neck and grabbing my breasts.

"The door is unlocked," I protested. Joey ripped at my clothing until my nightshirt was on the floor, and he had me pinned to the bed with him on top of me; he bit my nipples, and I tried to push him off me. "Please, Joey, not now, the girls," I demanded a little louder but still tried to be quiet so the girls would not hear what was happening. Joey had been drinking, and I could smell the strong odor of whiskey on his breath, and he was not taking no for an answer. It was like his body became so excited that he was not listening to my concerns at all. Joey held me down stronger and forced himself inside of me hard, and the tears welled up inside of me.

I couldn't help feeling like I was suddenly cheating on Jesse, but the more I tried to fight Joey off me, the more excited he became and the more force he used on me. He held my arms as he went down on me and bit my thighs between my legs, and his tongue was inside of me deeper and deeper, biting my clitoris until it felt like I was bleeding. I bit my tongue, trying not to scream out, and I finally just gave up the fight and just laid there and let him take whatever he wanted, praying that it would be over soon. I knew it wouldn't be, though, because he always lasted longer when drinking.

He let up on my arms and relaxed a little, and slowed his pace, so I took the chance to try and get away again, but as soon as I struggled to get loose, his excitement level rose again, and he was on top of me forcing me down on my face into the pillow, and he entered me from behind. He shoved himself inside me again and again until I felt like he was ripping me apart down there. I cried out, muffled in my pillow, and he became even crazier. He pulled my hair back, bit my neck, and stuck his fingers in my buttocks as he thrust himself deep inside me so that I felt a pain that I had never felt before. I lay there weeping hysterically on the pillow, which seemed like hours as he continued to tear at my body piece by piece.

Then suddenly, he flipped me over and slapped me in the face so hard that I felt dizzy and sick, and he flipped my legs up over my head and pushed himself inside me again, holding my hair and pinning my hands behind my head. "Can Jesse Fuck like this?" he yelled in his drunken rage. It was hopeless; I couldn't fight him. He was too powerful. I lay there broken as he raped me repeatedly until he finally laid still on top of me, and I knew he had finally passed out. I laid underneath him, which seemed like an hour before I slowly tried to push him off me, scared to wake him up, fearing that it would start all over again.

I slid out from underneath him, slipped my battered body to the floor, and crawled into the bathroom, holding back the tears. I wanted to take a hot bath so badly, but I was afraid the running water would wake him up, so I pulled on a pair of sweatpants and a sweatshirt. I tipped-toed out of the bedroom and quickly headed for the front door towards my car. The house was quiet, and I knew the girls must be sleeping by now, and I was relieved that they didn't hear my muffled screams. I got to the car and jumped in the driver's seat, and suddenly the tears came hard, and I cried hysterically. I couldn't stop crying and sat in the car for a long time before stopping. I started the car then and drove out to the hunting shack where I had been with Jesse.

I reached for my cell phone and called Jesse. He answered finally on the fifth ring, and I started bawling when I heard his voice. "Kally, what's wrong?" The sound of desperation and fear was in his voice. No matter how hard I tried, I couldn't get out any words. "Where are you?" He demanded. I finally told him the hunting shack over my uncontrollable sobs, and he hung up the phone quickly after he said he would be right there.

It was a matter of minutes when he rushed through the door with worry all over his face. I jumped to my feet, startled, and when I saw Jesse, I collapsed in his arms, sobbing violently again. He held me tightly, petting my hair and trying to soothe me before asking me again what had happened. I shook my head and tried to bury my head in his chest again, but he lifted my face with his hand under my chin, and he then saw the swollen cheek where Joey had hit me. "Kally," he said sternly, "Tell me what happened."

I blurted the whole thing out in a rush, and before I could finish, I could feel Jesse's body tensing up, and the color of his cheeks turned bright red with anger in his eyes. "I'll kill him!" He yelled, and he started for the door, but he stopped when I fell to the floor crying. He knelt beside me, held me again, and rocked me back and forth until I fell asleep in his arms out of pure exhaustion. Jesse was still holding me against him, lying on the small hunting cabin floor. I woke up to the birds singing outside and the sun shining through the small window.

His eyes were wide and glazed over, obviously deep in thought, and I cuddled closer to him. "Please let it go," I whispered desperately. He immediately rolled over and glared at me, "Oh my God, Kally, how can you ask me to do that?" He said with disbelief. "I don't know, but I just want to forget it all happened, and I don't want you to get involved or get hurt." I cried. "Please, Jesse," I begged. Jesse just shook his head and held me close again. "I love you, Kally, with all my heart, but I can't let it go; I just can't," He whispered firmly. "Please, Jesse, do this one thing for me," I pleaded again. He didn't answer me, he just held me, and we both closed our eyes and fell asleep again.

When I woke up again, Jesse was gone. I grabbed my purse, flew out the door, jumped in my car, and dialed his phone number as I sped down the road and back onto the highway. I just got his answering machine, and I pleaded into the phone. "Jesse, where are you? Please, Jesse, call me back! Don't do anything rash, Jesse, I beg you!" I hung up the phone and drove as fast as I dared to back to town. I pulled into the driveway, relieved that Jesse was not there. I was also relieved that Joey's truck was not in the driveway either.

I drove away again and headed towards the main street to check the café to see if Jesse was uptown. I could not find his truck anywhere. I drove past his house, and no one was home. I called several times, and no answer. Suddenly it dawned on me that Jesse knew that Joey was over at the ballpark doing some landscaping work. Oh God, I thought, don't let him be there. My body started to shake when I saw two police cars with their lights on and an ambulance sitting in the park. "Oh my God," I screamed. I parked the car, jumped out, and raced towards the ball field. I saw Jesse sitting in the back seat of the police car, and the ambulance was loading a gurney in the back. "What happened" I screamed. The officer looked at me and told me to stay back. "Is he dead?" I yelled.

"No, but he is in rough shape," the officer told me. Why didn't Jesse listen to me? Oh my God, now he was going to go to jail, and I would lose him. What if Joey dies? A million things were going through my mind, and panic overtook me. I raced to the police car and yelled, "Why Jesse, why did you do this" "I begged you not to," I cried.

Jesse put his head down with tears in his eyes and told me to go home. The police drove off with Jesse in the backseat, and I jumped back into my car and raced to the police station. I was in the police station trying to get an officer to talk to me, but everyone seemed to be running around too busy to notice I was even there. Finally, a familiar face came out, Mike Harris, the deputy sheriff. I knew he had grown up in town and went to school with Jesse.

"Mike," I jumped to my feet. "It's not good, Kally; I have to tell you that right away," he said, looking worried. "Joey is not in good shape, and Jesse isn't talking until his lawyer gets here," he told me. "Can I see him?" I asked Mike. He told me he would see what he could do about that, and apparently, Mike pulled some strings because he came out a few minutes later and said he would take me back to see him but only for a few minutes. Mike led me to a room, and when he opened the door, I saw Jesse sitting at a small table with his head down.

I rushed over to him quickly, and he held his hand out to push me back, "Go home, Kally, don't get involved in this" I gasped in disbelief. "Don't get involved?" I shrieked. "How can you tell me that? I am the reason this happened," I yelled at him. I wrapped my arms around his neck, crying then, and he held me close to him, caressing my hair. "Why didn't you listen to me, Jesse? Joey could die; he is in terrible shape," I told him.

"Good," he yelled. "That son of a bitch deserves to die," he said coldly. "Please, Jesse, don't say that! Not here! Talk with your lawyer, and don't say anything until you talk with him." I pleaded. Just then, Mike opened the door and told me that I had to go. I hugged Jesse and kissed him gently, with tears rolling down my face. "It will be okay, Kally, go home and get rest." I left him there with his head down, looking at the floor, and Mike shut the door and locked it behind us. "Go home, Kally, and I will call you when I hear anything" Mike hugged me, and I left for home. I could not believe this was happening.

I walked into the house, and the girls were at the kitchen table waiting to hear what had happened. They had already heard that Joey had been taken to the hospital severely beaten to near death. "Mom, what is going on? What happened?" Carrie rushed towards me, hugging me. I told her that Joey and Jesse had gotten into a fight and that Jesse was now in jail, and they weren't sure if Joey would survive. "Oh my God," Carrie shrieked again.

Jenni was still sitting at the table, and she didn't have much of a response to the news. I looked at her, wondering why she seemed not affected by the information, and she looked up at me with tears in her eyes. Jenni was quiet and hid her feelings deep inside sometimes, and I never knew exactly what was going through her mind.

Finally, after a few minutes, she looked up again at me and said, "He hurt you, didn't he, Mom?" I looked down, not wanting to cry, and Carrie chimed in, "What are you talking about, Jenni?" "Who hurt her?" Then Carrie looked at me and demanded answers. "What aren't you telling us, Mom?" "What the hell happened?" I could no longer hold back the tears in my eyes, and I broke down and told the girls what had happened. Jenni said she had heard me cry out, but she was not sure if she should interrupt or not. She was crying then, and I hugged her, assuring her that none of it was her fault.

"Well, he deserves to die then," Carrie screamed out. "Please, honey, don't say that; no one deserves to die," I told her. After a while, I calmed both girls down and went to lie on the couch to rest. I was drained and scared. I did not know what would happen next, and my mind wouldn't shut off. I awoke to the phone ringing and jumped up to answer it quickly. "Kally," Mike said with sadness and concern in his voice, and I already knew what he was going to tell me before he even said the words. "Joey died a few minutes ago" I dropped the phone and sank to my knees, crying intensely. Carrie rushed into the room, picked up the phone, briefly talked to Mike, and hung up. She knelt beside me and hugged me. "I am so sorry, Mom," she said, holding my hand.

The prosecuting officers decided to charge Jesse with first-degree murder, saying that Jesse went to the park that day with the intent to Kill Joey after learning that Joey had raped his friend. Jesse's lawyer convinced them to drop it to manslaughter after evidence showed that Jesse went to the park out of anger and rage and had full intent to beat Joey up, but he did not intend to kill him. Joey had apparently had a knife and had taken it out to fight Jesse off, and when both men lunged and rolled around on the ground, one of the other contractors witnessed the whole thing and stated that Joey had fallen on the knife. Thank God for that witness that testified, or I don't know what would have happened to Jesse.

The trial lasted for six months, and the judge sentenced Jesse to six years in prison, and I only saw him at the trial and once before they hauled him away. I told him I would wait for him, but he snapped at me and told me to get on with my life and that he didn't want me to come and visit him. "That is ridiculous, Jesse; you are going to need me now more than ever," I told him. "No, Kally, don't come," he demanded again. I tried to kiss him goodbye, and he pushed me towards the door, not looking at me. I thought he would come to his senses, but for six years, I tried to see him, and for six years, he refused my visits. The post office returned my unopened letters.

I was devastated and hurt. I felt like I had lost my best friend. I poured myself into my work and shut out the rest of the world. Carrie came to visit often during her breaks at school, but I couldn't bring myself out of this slump of depression that I had sunk into so deeply. Jenni stayed busy with sports and school, and I did manage to go to her basketball games, but I left and went home as soon as they were over and avoided talking with anyone. I couldn't understand how Jesse could just shut me out after all we had been through together.

CHAPTER TWELVE

TIME PASSES BY-GUILT SETS IN

Carrie had come home for Thanksgiving that final year before Jesse was to get out of prison, and she announced that she had accepted her boyfriend Todd's marriage proposal. I hugged her tightly and tried my best to be happy for her. I suddenly snapped out of my slump and began making wedding plans with Carrie. She was so beautiful, and I was very happy for her.

She had been dating Todd for three years, and he was a wonderful man I knew would always be there for her. I always thought that Carrie and Josh would end up together, but when they went to different colleges, they stayed in touch as friends but drifted apart romantically. I had heard that Josh met a gal out in California and was also engaged to be married. Carrie and Todd had met at a college football game, and they both hit it off right from the beginning and have been inseparable ever since. The two seem so right for each other that they reminded me of Mike and me when we first met. They moved into an apartment together about two hours south of Springfield. The news of their wedding plans gave me something exciting to focus on and brought me some positivity in my life.

After Jenni had graduated from high school, she decided to attend the University of Wisconsin in Maddison, which was only about half an hour away. Still, she wanted the whole college life experience, so she chose to live in the dorms. I was truly alone now, but the girls visited often. Maggie had attended Jenni's graduation ceremony and party just like she had promised, and it was great to see her again. She had sold Ali's house and still lived next door but told me she was also thinking about selling her house and moving to Chicago, where she had lived before moving to help Ali out. Maggie loved the big city and could get a better job and escape the loss she felt every time she looked at Ali's house. It devastated her not to see her sitting on her porch swing anymore.

We had Carrie and Todd's wedding in July, and I walked Carrie down the aisle, holding her hand proudly. She wore a beautiful white wedding dress with pearls down her back, and her skin was tanned and pure. Jenni walked down the aisle as her matron of honor and looked stunning. At the dance, Carrie came and took my hand to dance with me, and she whispered, "Mom, I wanted to let you know that Jesse sent me a card wishing me a wonderful life and told me to make sure I take care of my mom" I gasped in surprise. "He still loves you, Mamma," she said with a smile, and I held back the tears. I missed him so much and thought I would never see him again, but now I had hope that I was still in his heart, and this was just yet another obstacle we had to overcome. I wondered how Jesse even knew where Carrie lived to send her a card, but then I realized that he probably was still in touch with his sister and obtained information from her. Why wouldn't he reach out to me? I thought to myself.

Two months after the wedding, Carrie and Todd came home on a special visit to let me know that they were expecting a baby and I would be a gramma. I was so thrilled that I threw my arms around Carrie and Todd and hugged them so tightly that they were laughing, trying to catch their breath. I immediately started buying baby clothes and baby things, not knowing if they would have a boy or a girl. Carrie told me she wanted to name the baby Michael after her father if it was a boy. I smiled and hugged her, letting her know that I thought that was an excellent idea, and told her how proud her father would have been of her and how he would have loved Todd.

Jesse's release date was coming up on November 28th, and I wanted to be waiting at the gate when they released him. I awoke that morning, fixed my hair, and carefully put my makeup on. I slipped on a pair of jeans and a black sweater and took one last look in the mirror, deciding that I looked pretty nice and Jesse would like it. That day there was already a lot of snow on the ground, and it looked like the roads might be icy, so I wanted to get an early start. I drove the long drive to the prison and waited at the gate for his release, and when I looked at the clock and realized it was already

11 am, I wondered why he wasn't coming out the doors. I got on my cell phone and called the prison and asked about Jesse's release, and they told me that he was released at 6:30 am before I had even arrived.

I wondered where he had gone and who had picked him up. I couldn't get a hold of him on a phone that was no longer in service for the last six years, and I had no idea how to contact him. Where did he go? I wondered. I drove the long drive home with tears in my eyes, wondering if I would ever see him again and devastated that Jesse could just walk away from me without saying goodbye again.

The days went by slowly, and I poured myself into my work again. I asked around town about Jesse wondering if anyone else had heard anything about his whereabouts. The townspeople that once cared so much for this guy acted like he was someone that didn't deserve their time. They treated me like it was all my fault, and I lost a lot of friends along the way due to my depressive state of mind. I guess they decided to give up on me after I showed them no sense of wanting to be social over the last six years. They didn't understand the full depth of what I had gone through, and I didn't care to share it with any of them, so I just continued working and going home to my empty, lonely house.

I was tired of sitting alone in the house, so I took some photography classes at the high school. I also made frequent visits to see Carrie and to help her prepare for her new arrival. The morning that little Mikayla came into our lives was among my proudest. I became a grandma on April 26th, 2004, and she was quite a bundle of cuteness. I was up for a visit, and at 7:30 am, I was stretching in bed, trying to wake up, when I heard the commotion coming from Carrie and Todd's room. I came out in the hallway just as Todd came rushing out in a panic, white-colored face looking at me as if confused and bewildered. I knew it was time to bring that little one into the world.

"Grab Carrie's overnight bag and put it in the car; I will get her ready to go," I calmly told him. He nodded his head and stood there in shock, I urged him to go quickly, and he darted down the stairs.

As I entered her room, I saw her sitting on the edge of the bed, looking very uncomfortable. "Hi, honey. Are you ready to go to the hospital?" She nodded and gave me half a smile. "I'm scared, Mamma," she told me. I wrapped my arms around her and gently helped her to her feet. "It's going to be the best day of your life, honey; you're going to be a mother" I walked her to the door, and she laid her head on my shoulder. "Thank you, mamma, for being here" I smiled, and we drove to the hospital.

Todd filled out some paperwork while I got Carrie settled into bed, and the nurse checked her to see her progress. "Not long to go," the nurse reported, "you've dilated to seven already. Todd came in, and I told them I would be in the waiting room waiting for the wonderful news. Todd grabbed my hand, "Don't go; please stay with us," he pleaded with a nervous smile. I nodded and stood by their side as I watched my little girl have a baby of her own.

Watching your child go through so much pain was tough, but it was the most beautiful experience of my life, watching my grandchild enter this world. Todd held Mikayla as I held Carrie's hand and told her how proud I was of her. We weren't in the recovery room long when Jenni burst through the door. "Where's the baby? Is it over?" she said anxiously and looked around the room until she spotted her little niece lying in the hospital bassinet, fast asleep. "Oh my, she is so tiny and so beautiful; look at all her dark hair" She was in awe over her little baby niece. Jenni quickly kissed her sister and told her she did great.

Carrie fell asleep then, Todd stayed with her, and Jenni and I went back to Carrie's house for a rest. It was an exceptionally long morning. Out of habit, I reached for my phone to dial Jesse's number, as I did a hundred times before in the last six years, but sadly put it back in my purse when I realized I had no way of reaching him to tell him of my news. He was always the one I could call to talk to about anything, and I missed him so much. I lay down on the couch at Carrie's and drifted off to sleep immediately.

When I woke up, the sun was down, and I was surprised I had slept so long. I heard a noise in the kitchen, and I went to see what Jenni was doing. "Hi, mamma, you were sleeping so soundly, I didn't have the heart to wake you," Jenni said with a smile. "Are you okay, Mamma?" she always called me Mamma. "I am fine, Jenni; why?" I asked. Jenni shrugged her shoulders and turned towards the stove to stir the hamburger meat she was frying up for the spaghetti she was making. "Jenni, I am fine," I said again when I could tell she was still worried. Jenni turned around again and looked at me with questioning eyes.

"It's just that I heard you call out his name when you were sleeping," she said. "Who?" I asked, surprised. "Jesse," she said, staring at me and waiting for my response. I told her again that I was okay and that I just missed him and wondered where he was and if he was okay. "I am just so used to calling him and telling him when exciting things happen in my life, and I must have been thinking about him and wanting to tell him that I became a Gramma today" I looked down at the table and fidgeted with my hands, hoping that she accepted that answer and the conversation would end there.

She seemed to be satisfied with that because she came over and gave me a quick hug. "I am sure Jesse is fine, Mamma, and he will call you again; I know he will," she said, trying to cheer me up. I nodded, got up, returned to the living room, and turned on the television. I snuggled on the couch in a fuzzy blanket and waited for Jenni to finish cooking the spaghetti on the stove. I was hungry and ready to eat.

I stayed for a few more days and helped Carrie with the baby when she came home from the hospital. Jenni had to get back to school, and she gave us all a hug goodbye and told us she would keep in touch. As Jenni was getting in her car, she excitedly hollered back to us, "By the way, I met someone, and I will be bringing him home to meet you for Thanksgiving" She jumped into her car and drove off with a smile and a wave leaving us all standing there with our mouths open wide. I looked at Carrie and Todd and started laughing.

"She did that on purpose," Carrie reported. I nodded and smiled again. Jenni was like that. She did not want to take away Carrie and Todd's excitement by becoming the center of attention.

Jenni didn't want us all bombarding her with questions, either. She would tell us in her own time, and I knew this man must be pretty special to her if she was telling us about him at all. Jenni was private and only shared things readily if they were important to her.

I loaded the car that morning to head back home, and I was all sad and choked up inside to be leaving. I held the baby for a long time that morning and petted her little face. "I am your Gramma, and I am going to come to visit you whenever I can and spoil you, rotten little girl," I told her as I kissed her soft little cheeks. I handed her back to Carrie, and she gave the baby to Todd, grabbed me, and hugged me tightly, both of us sobbing now. "We will visit more often, Mom, I promise," she told me and kissed me goodbye. I glanced back, and both were standing in the yard waving to me as the tears rolled down our faces. My little girl was all grown up with a baby of her own. I felt so lonely on that day I drove home.

I checked the mail at the post office as soon as I pulled into town, and like usual, there were only bills to go through. I drove up to my empty little house and parked the car, sitting there thinking awhile. I thought about selling my home and getting something smaller since I was all alone now, but how could I sell this house that my children grew up in? We made such beautiful memories in this home. I convinced myself that this house also had terrible memories as I thought about the night that Joey changed all our lives in his drunken state of mind. Tears came to my eyes as I thought about that awful night, the tragedy that occurred, and the years I spent without Jesse. I wondered if Jesse and I would be together now if he had listened to me and left Joey alone.

I quickly shrugged it off and wiped the tears away. I went in and started unpacking and sorting my dirty laundry, immediately throwing it into the washing machine. I checked the answering machine, and it was flashing one message. It was Cathy. I hadn't heard from her in a while and assumed she blamed me for Joey's death just like the rest of the town seemed to.

"Kally, please call me. I have not heard from you in forever, you seem to vanish off the face of the earth, and I miss you, my friend, so please call." The message was a nice one. I picked up the phone and called her. She answered and began chatting a hundred miles an hour, just like she had to catch me up on everything that had been happening since I seemed to vanish. I started laughing and then told her I had become a gramma. Again, she started chattering about how exciting that was, and she didn't stop talking to take a breath. Finally, I asked her to have lunch with me tomorrow, and she agreed. I figured that was the only way I would get off the phone with her, and I hung up laughing.

I showered, dressed, and hurried out the door the following day. I was surprised I still had a job after how much time I had taken off. Still, Ella had given me control of everything, including making my own hours and delegating duties while I was away. I grabbed a bagel with cream cheese and a cup of coffee and flew out the door. I knew my desk would be plump full of things that I needed to catch up on, and I was right; it was. My coworkers seemed glad that I was finally back. A bouquet of Carnations in a beautiful glass vase sat on my desk, and a balloon read, "Welcome back." "Thank you," I told them as they all stared at me and smiled. I began working and catching up on answering all my missed messages.

Most of them, to my surprise, were people from town telling me congratulations on becoming a gramma. I thought to myself, "Hmm, maybe it was only my imagination that everyone blamed me, and perhaps it was me that pulled myself away from people and buried myself away and alone.

CHAPTER THIRTEEN

THE DARK SIDE

Cathy came bolting through the door right at noon. "Hey," she came running to me with arms open wide and embraced me with a big hug. "Come on, grab your purse and tell me all about that new bundle of joy in your life," she started pulling me towards the door as I reached for my purse. I pulled away after a second and told her it was great to see her.

We had a wonderful lunch at the café, and everyone who came in the door who had heard about Carrie having a baby all told me how happy they were for me. I couldn't believe the warm welcome I was getting from everyone, and I told Cathy how surprised I was. "Oh my God, Kally, they have all been waiting for you to join the living again," she exclaimed rather boldly. "It has been you that has gone into hiding for the last six years, and we all thought that you would come out of it when Jesse came back, but" ....

"Wait, what do you mean when Jesse came back?" I interrupted her abruptly. By the look on my face, she could tell I was surprised and didn't know anything about Jesse.

"Oh, you didn't know? She asked. "He was back last week and cleaned out the things that he had left at his sister's house. I just assumed that he had gotten in touch with you" She looked apologetic. I suddenly told her I had to go and grabbed my purse, and darted for the door before the tears could fall. She told me how sorry she was, and I jumped in my car and sped away as fast as possible. I called work and explained that I wasn't coming back this afternoon, and I went home, curled up on the couch, and cried.

Why wouldn't he contact me? Did he blame me for Joey's death? Did he blame me for the last six years of his life in prison? He must hate me now, and I wished I could talk to him, but he was avoiding me. I cried myself to sleep, and when I woke up, it was 2 am.

The house was quiet, and I was no longer tired, so I made myself a cup of hot cocoa and went outside on the porch swing to drink it. I thought about Jesse and how I longed to talk to him again. How could he blame me for everything when I begged him to drop it and leave Joey alone? He didn't listen to me, which is why he spent six years in prison. How could he possibly blame me for that? I thought.

I had to get on with my life and bury all this pain behind me. It was disrupting my whole life and tearing me apart piece by piece. Jesse had disappeared after he got out of prison, and it had been three years without a word from him, so I had to do something to leave it behind me. It is evident that he had moved on, so I decided that I was going to relocate to another town and start over. I would dig out the old map, close my eyes and pick my new destination. I would begin again somewhere nice where nobody knew me. I went back to bed, pleased with my decision.

I went to work the next day feeling better as I thought about which town I would pick, but I suddenly felt lonely and afraid. I wasn't getting any younger, and when I started fresh last time, I had the girls to get me through the loneliness. Now it would just be me, not knowing anyone or having anyone. At the age of 48, I would have to start a new job and find a new home in a town where nobody knew me. I would have to make new friends again. I would miss Cathy, and I would miss my job terribly. I should rethink my decision, I thought to myself.

The phone rang, startling me from my thoughts, and it was Cathy. "Kally, go to Jesse's sister's house right now," she demanded. "He is there now, and it is time that the two of you work this whole thing out and you get some answers before it destroys your whole life," she said. I hung up, set my phone to the answering machine, explained quickly to the girls in the office, and flew out the door.

I pulled up to the old white house and immediately saw Jesse in the window. I walked, no half ran up the walk, and banged on the front door with force. The door opened, and Jesse stood in front of me, looking like a beaten man. His face was sad but angered. He looked like he was in desperate need of a shave, and he didn't smile when he saw me. "Why are you here?" he said with a stern, gruff voice. "You shouldn't be here, Kally; I thought I made that perfectly clear to you."

"Clear to me!" I screamed at him, stopping him dead in his tracks. "What the hell do you mean, made it clear to me?" "You have avoided me, returned my letters, and erased me completely from your life without so much as a small explanation whatsoever, so what the hell do you mean that you made it clear to me?" I stopped and started in again before he could even answer me.

I let him have it with both barrels and told him exactly how my life was during those six years he was in prison and how it has been since the day he walked out of those prison doors without contacting me. How I had to deal with the loss of him and how I had to deal with all the guilt of knowing that it was all my fault that he killed a man and how I pulled myself out of existence and talked to no one because my very best friend in the whole world walked out of my life without so much as a goodbye.

He stood there without expression listening to me rant and rave. When I finished screaming at him, the tears came, and my body started shaking and losing control of my ability to stand up. Jesse grabbed me before I stumbled to the ground. He pressed me tight against his chest, and I struck him with my fists against his chest, sobbing hysterically. His face suddenly softened, and tears were in his eyes.

"Kally, I didn't mean to hurt you, honey," he said softly. "I meant to protect you" I looked up at him, wondering how any of this protected me. "I couldn't let you live a life with me knowing that I was a convicted felon and my life as I knew it was over. I couldn't let you go through what I had gone through since that awful day when I took a man's life. The shame of what I did, and every time you would look at me, you would remember what I did." The tears in his eyes made me crumble and hold him closer. He brushed the hair from my face and told me to go home. "Please, Kally, just go home and live your life" he suddenly pushed me away, and the softness faded from his face.

I then noticed his sister standing in the living room with a blonde woman whom I didn't know. The blonde woman stared at me, looking like she didn't like me, and I suddenly realized that this woman must be with Jesse. His sister also had tears in her eyes and looked at me with sympathetic eyes. The blonde woman stepped forward and reached for Jesse's hand, but he pulled it away, not wanting to hurt me anymore. I wiped the tears from my eyes and told him I was sorry for bothering him, and I ran to my car and sped away. Again, I went home and spent the rest of the afternoon on my couch in tears, but this time they were angry tears.

I tried hard that night to put him out of my mind telling myself that he was a fool for thinking that he was trying to protect me and that I wouldn't think about what happened if he wasn't in my life. I thought about what happened every day of my life regardless, and the guilt I felt was unbearable. I thought if I wouldn't have told Jesse, none of this would have even happened, so how could I not blame myself for all of it?

For the next couple of weeks, I poured myself into my work and spent no extra time visiting with anyone. I was distant and cold to my coworkers, who were very understanding and sympathetic to me as Cathy filled them all in on what had happened, at least as far as she knew what had happened. I told her nothing, either. The girls would call me on the phone, and I talked to them and tried hard to listen to all their life's joys and all about my new grandchild, but they could tell I was not myself. I had heard that Jesse and his girlfriend were renting a place about 30 miles away now, and I prayed that I would never run into him again because it hurt too much to see him.

After a few months of hiding, it was time to get out of my slump, so I called Cathy and invited her to lunch. Over lunch with Cathy, she told me she wanted me to meet her cousin, who was coming to town. I protested right away, knowing what she was up to, but she put her finger to my lips to hush me, "Kally, it's not a setup, I promise; I just want you to come out with us and have some fun. I am doing this more for him." She told me. "He just went through a divorce after being married for 30 years, and he is having a real hard time with moving on" I reluctantly agreed to go out with them for dinner on Saturday night.

That evening I showered, got ready to go out, and rummaged through my closet, trying to figure out what to wear. I finally chose a black silk blouse with white jeans and topped myself off with jewelry and a scarf. I took one last look in the mirror and was about to change again when the doorbell rang, and I knew I had run out of time. I ran down to open the door, and Cathy hugged me, "You look great; Let's go," she demanded. I walked out to the car, and the door opened, and a tall man with dark hair and dark eyes, reasonably good-looking, got out to let me in the car.

"This is Jim; Jim, this is Kally," Cathy said anxiously, looking at both of us for some love-at-first-sight reaction. I smiled and shook his hand, "It is very nice to meet you," He shook my hand and told me the same. We arrived at the Shepard Inn for dinner reservations at 6:oo sharp.

We sat at our table with candles lit and cinnamon smelling up the room. It was a dimly lit restaurant with quiet secluded tables set off in separate spaces for privacy. Soft music came from the speakers scattered around the ceiling, and beautiful trees and flowers spread throughout the dining area. People were chattering quietly amongst themselves. It reminded me of the Shanty where I had worked in California, and I wondered how Josh was doing. I felt awful for not keeping in touch with him, but life gets busy, and I washed that part of my life away.

The waiter came to take our order, and Jim took it upon himself to order a bottle of his favorite wine for us to all taste. I could tell right away that Jim was a take-control kind of guy but seemed like a real gentleman. I ordered the Steak and shrimp dinner, and he immediately suggested I try their shrimp linguine. "Thank you, but I prefer the steak and shrimp," I said kindly but slightly annoyed that he didn't think I could order my dinner. By the look on his face, he didn't seem to like my response either.

We all made small talk, with Cathy doing most of the talking, and she kept looking at both Jim and me for any chemistry between us. That was annoying, and I wanted to give her a kick underneath the table to suggest that she knock it off, but I refrained from doing so.

After dinner, we all ordered a drink and went into the bar area to watch the one-person band that had started. The man was a singer, and he also was a comedian and quite funny. We sat at a table by the bar and sipped on our drinks. I was relieved that the entertainment kept the conversation to a bare minimum at our table. When Jim reached for my hand to ask me to dance, I immediately refused, thinking that this wasn't the place to get up and dance and that I would feel very uncomfortable doing so.

Again, he rolled his eyes, looking frustrated with me, and I shrugged it off, not really caring what he thought. I noticed then that Cathy seemed on edge and uncomfortable, and her eyes kept looking behind me. I started to turn to see what was irritating her, but she quickly grabbed my arm and tried to make conversation. I raised my eyebrows, thinking she had lost her mind, and I instantly turned around to discover her problem.

Jesse was standing at the entrance with his girlfriend, and I don't think he even saw us sitting inside. My heartbeat was faster, and my cheeks felt flushed. "Kally, forget it; just don't look over there," she told me. Cathy's husband saw the fuss and told me to act like I didn't even see him. Jim had no clue what was going on but soon figured it was all about the guy that we kept turning to look at. "Now do you want to dance?" he said smugly. "NO, I do not want to dance, Jim," I said coldly. He rolled his eyes at me again, and I just wanted to run out of there as fast as I could, but I kept myself seated in my chair.

"Oh God, they are walking this way," Cathy said, looking very nervous and uncomfortable. I thought, what is she worried about? Why does it bother her so much? I am the one that should be irritated and nervous; after all, here is the man that I have loved for so long in my life and was with his girlfriend at the same bar as I was. I am the one that has to look at him with another woman and see how happy she makes him and how miserable I feel with this man that is so rude that I just met. By the look on my face, it is evident that I am unhappy and not having a good time.

Just then, a man grabbed my arm, swooped me up from behind, and hugged me. I was shocked, but when I got to my feet, I saw Sam's son, Brody, standing before me.

"Kally," he said as he hugged me tightly. He whispered in my ear, "It's going to be okay, girl; just show him how happy you are and how your life is going just fine without him" I smiled with my eyes slightly tearing up, and he held me closer. "He doesn't know what he's missing, baby, and if he does, then he isn't happy either," he said softly in my ear again. He hugged me for a long time, rocking me back and forth, letting the whole place know how good it was to see me again, and it had been too long since we had seen each other last. I couldn't help but start laughing then thinking that Brody and I never were that close and how we see each other all the time in passing and barely speak to each other. Still, he acted like we were just the most fabulous friends, all for the benefit of taking the heart-sick look off my face for Jesse to witness.

"He notices you now, honey," he whispered again, and then Brody sat down at our table with us and told me not to look his way again, and he smiled and gave me a wink. Cathy knew what was going on, and she smiled in approval. Jim looked annoyed at Brody sitting down with us uninvited but very welcome. "He is definitely looking this way, and it seems the girlfriend is slightly annoyed with him," he spoke quietly as he cheered my glass of wine and acted like we all were just in our own little world having a wonderful time; I laughed again and started to have a great time finally.

After a while, the conversation started flowing at the table. I mostly talked with Brody, and I wasn't as distracted by the presence of Jesse in the same place as I was. Don't get me wrong; I was highly aware that he was only about 40 feet away from me. Still, I did precisely what Brody told me to do, and that was not to look at Jesse or show him that I even noticed that he was there. At about midnight, I announced that I should be getting home. Cathy objected that she didn't want to leave yet, so Brody offered to drive me home.

Jim immediately rolled his eyes and said he could take me home, but Brody reached for my hand and rose to his feet. "it's okay; I am going right past her place; I can take her. "I reached for my purse and looked at Jim, and smiled, "Thank you all for the wonderful evening, and it was very nice meeting you, Jim," I said as I stood up to leave with Brody still holding my hand and pulling the chair out for me to get through. Jim just nodded, displeased with the outcome of the evening, and Cathy told me she'd call me tomorrow. Brody slipped his arm around me and led me toward the door. I realized he was still giving Jesse a show because he pulled me closer and whispered, "He is watching you like a hawk, baby" I leaned in closer and laughed at his comment.

When we got outside the restaurant, Brody cracked up laughing. "Wow, was that ever fun! You should have seen his face, Kally! He was fuming with jealousy, and his girlfriend grabbed his face to keep him from staring at our table. She was furious with him!" he said excitedly and pleased with his accomplishment. He kept laughing, and I laughed too. "That was a lot of fun, Brody, and thank you; I needed that," I told him. He opened the car door to let me in and closed it behind me. He slipped the valet a tip and stood in front of the car, chatting with the guy for a while.

I suddenly looked at Brody and noticed that he was handsome. He had a tight shirt on that showed his dark, tanned skin and muscular body. His smile showed his perfect teeth, and his dark brown eyes glowed enthusiastically. I thought he was younger than me by about ten years, and I quickly shook off any thoughts I might be having at that moment. I brushed it off, thinking that I was just lonely and the drinks I had that night went to my head.

He jumped in the driver's seat and sped away from the curb. He started to talk to me about Jesse again, and I just shook my head. "Can we please not talk about him anymore, Brody? It was a fun evening, but I need to get Jesse off my mind" He smiled, took my hand, and agreed. "Sorry, Kally. He pulled up to my place, jumped out of the car, and ran around to open my door, which surprised me. He held out his hand, helped me to my feet, and walked me to the door like a fine gentleman. "You deserve better, Kally," he said with a smile and leaned in and kissed me lightly on the cheek.

"Have dinner with me this weekend, Kally," he blurted out. Without even thinking about it twice, I agreed, and he gave me a quick hug, "Pick you up at 6?" he asked. I smiled and agreed. I went inside my big empty house, closed the door behind me, and watched out the window as he drove away.

I suddenly began to wonder what I was doing. Was I really interested in going out with Brody, or was I just flattered by the whole evening of him rescuing me in front of Jesse and his girlfriend? I shrugged it off and went to bed. I awoke to the telephone ringing, rolled over, rubbed my sleepy eyes, and looked at the clock. 4 am, what the hell? Who on earth could be calling me this time of the morning? I thought and worried about the girls. I answered the phone in a panic.

"Kally, don't hang up; I need to talk to you," Jesse said quickly, pleading with me. "Jesse? What is wrong?" I asked, still worrying. "Can I come over?" he asked. "I need to talk to you," he pleaded again. "It's not a good idea, Jesse; what do you want to tell me?" I told him, knowing that If I let him come over, my heart would crumble all over again. But he begged me to let him come over and talk, and something in his voice made me change my mind, and I agreed to let him come over. I met him outside on the porch and didn't invite him inside. He hurried up the sidewalk, grabbed me around my waist, and pulled me to him, hugging me. I pushed him back harshly and yelled at him, "Don't do this to me" What is it you want to talk about?" I demanded rather sternly then.

"Kally, seeing you tonight, I, I," his voice drifted, unable to get the words out. "What is it, Jesse?" I snarled. His eyes welled up with tears, and he spoke the words that melted my heart repeatedly. I was afraid of this, and I knew I should have never let him come over. He had been drinking, and his hands kept finding ways to touch me. I kept pushing him back repeatedly until my heart couldn't stand it anymore, and I let him pull me close to him, and I started crying on his chest. He smoothed my hair with his hands, "Shhhh, honey; it's okay. I miss you so much, Kally! I lost my best friend, and it's killing me inside." He told me. I looked up at his eyes and could feel the pain that he felt inside because I was feeling it too, but I was so angry at him. Why couldn't I push him away and tell him to go home? I thought. His mouth came down on mine, and we were locked together instantly, not wanting to release each other and both wanting to feel again. Jesse picked me up in his arms and carried me in the house, and we made it as far as the Foyer before we crumbled to the floor and started tearing each other's clothing off.

Jesse was on top of me, kissing my neck, and his hands searched for every part of my body as if he had never been there before. He touched every place on my body, exploring it as if it were the first time, and I screamed out in pleasure and let myself feel for the first time in a very long time. After we both felt our bodies release and explode in pleasure, we lay on the floor in each other's arms and started laughing. All of a sudden, my laughter turned into tears.

"Kally honey, what's wrong?" Jesse leaned over to me and put his chin on my neck, kissing me sweetly. "Why do we keep doing this to each other, Jesse? We need to stop this and move on with our lives," I told him. "We keep hurting each other over and over again," I said. "It's all going to be okay, honey; we will move away together, put the past all behind us, and be together again. I promise you that," he told me. "When Jesse?" I said and sat up, looking him in the eye. "Soon," he told me, gently pulling me on top of him and kissing me hard on my mouth again, sending my body in full throttle all over again.

We made love again, and this time we made it to the bedroom, and afterward, I fell asleep in Jesse's arms. It was the way it should be, I thought. A few hours later, the sun was shining in my window, and the birds were chirping outside, and I rolled over to look at the clock and realized that Jesse was gone. "Was it just a dream? I thought. No, it was not a dream, Jesse was really here, and he left again, leaving me empty and lonely inside. Would he return? Would he keep his promise, and would we be together soon? I asked myself even though I knew what the answer was already. No, he would go back to his life and put me out of his mind again, leaving   me   hurting   inside   all   over   again

CHAPTER FOURTEEN

HEARTS CONNECTED

I got up and started making coffee, and as it was brewing, I went to shower and get cleaned up. I pulled on my bathrobe, went back out to the kitchen, and sat at the kitchen table with my coffee, and the tears didn't come this time as I sat there thinking about the night before. I was angry for allowing my heart to soften again regarding Jesse. I went back into my room and threw on a pair of jeans and a sweatshirt, and then I found the note on my nightstand. It read,

"Dear Kally, I have missed you so much, and last night was amazing being with you again, holding you in my arms again, and making love to you. I lied next to you and watched you sleep, and I realized that you and I seem to fit like a glove together, but I wish I could be more for you. The things I have done over the last few years are not forgivable; you deserve so much more than me. Every time I look at you reminds me of the pain I have caused you and many other people. I can't be in this town without constant reminders. I have to say goodbye once and for all, my love, but remember I am always watching over you, and I will be here for you in a second whenever you need me. One day I pray that we will be together. I was not lying when I said I wanted to move away and be with you, but I can't expect you to give up your life to be with me."

I love you, sweet girl. Always and forever, Jesse

I crumbled the letter in my hand and threw it on the bed; still, the tears never came. I was angry and wished I knew where to find Jesse because I would go to him now and let him have it with both barrels. How could he play with my heart like that and walk away? I thought. I am 48 years old, and I have wasted so much time waiting for him to come to his senses, waiting for us to have our chance at happiness, but I am sick of waiting for him and sick of pain. I am sick to death of him using the same excuse repeatedly as to why he can't be in my life as a constant. Right then, I decided to go on that date with Brody, forget about Jesse, visit my daughters more often, and put my life back on track again.

I called Brody that afternoon and left a message on his voice mail letting him know that I was looking forward to our dinner on Saturday night, but I had a change of plans and to call me. Brody called me that Tuesday evening. I told him I needed to cancel our Saturday night dinner because I wanted to go away for the weekend and see my daughter and granddaughter. He was disappointed, but then I asked if he would like to join me and go away for the weekend, and he agreed. I went to work that Monday and decided I would get a lot done this week and then take off on Friday. I told Brody to meet me at my place around 8:30 am on Friday, and he agreed. I was excited to see Carrie and Todd, and my granddaughter. Mikayla was walking now and talking; it had been so long since I could visit.

Carrie was excited when I told her I was coming. She called Jenni and invited her over with her boyfriend, Jim, whom I had only met once because he was a busy construction worker. Brody met me at my place on Friday afternoon, and we began our weekend. I told Carrie that I was bringing Brody with me, and to my surprise, Carrie said that sounded great, and she didn't ask any questions about it before hanging up. Our drive to Carrie's would allow Brody and me to get to know each other better by getting out of town without prying, watchful eyes everywhere. Brody arrived on time and helped me carry my luggage to the car.

Brody was kind, and he was a gentleman. Sam and Ella raised him to be a fine young man. He was younger than I was, but he never acted like he was. We had a lot to talk about, and he always treated me like a lady. He asked if he could drive, and I gladly handed him my keys. The conversation went smoothly the whole 2-hour drive, and I found him to be very charming, intelligent, and kind. The weekend was relaxing, and it was nice to see the girls again. My baby granddaughter grew so much. Mikayla was beautiful. Her long hair was shiny, and her dark eyes had a sparkle in them that had a naughty streak a mile long, but it was cute, mischievous, and hard not to laugh when she looked at you with those pouty full lips of hers. When we left that Sunday, I said a tearful goodbye to the girls, and Jenni told me that Jim had asked her to get married, but she wasn't ready yet. I didn't know what she was waiting for, as they had been together for about three years, but I respected her decision and didn't pry. She seemed to have her head on straight and knew what she wanted, and I envied that about her but was so proud of how grown up she was too.

On the way home, we stopped at a roadside truck stop for lunch and sat in the booth waiting for our food. I thought about Jesse and our last night together. I still didn't quite understand his thought process, which made me so angry. It must have shown on my face because Brody interrupted my thoughts when he said, "Kally, what is troubling you?" I looked into his beautiful brown eyes, half smiled at him, and apologized for not paying attention and drifting away. "I know you're thinking about Jesse, and I also know that you aren't going to get him off your mind anytime soon, but I hope that you will give me a chance to show you that you can love me like that someday, too," he told me with sadness in his eyes. I shook my head and smiled.

"Brody, I will be frank with you. I do not want to love anyone else like that again. It is not normal for one thing. Jesse and I have hurt each other so much over the years; that can't be love. Love should not hurt so much." I explained to him. "Well, Kally, the two of you have loved each other and will always love each other, but it's hard for Jesse to forgive himself for his actions. Jesse doesn't think he is good enough for you, but it's hard for him to think anyone else is good enough for you, either. Jesse wants you to be happy, but yet he doesn't think anyone is good enough to make you happy and treat you the way you deserve, including himself," He continued, just like he knew some deep secret about our relationship like no one else knew and I listened to him attentively believing his words and trying to make sense of it all.

Brody talked openly about his feelings and read people, almost like he should have been a therapist. I just shook my head and told him I didn't want to talk about it any longer. We paid for our lunch and finished the trip back home quietly.

When Brody pulled up into my driveway, he reached for my hand before I could get out and said he enjoyed the weekend with me very much. "I know it will take time, and I know you will never truly let go of Jesse in your heart, but I hope that you and I can become closer," he told me. Brody was a sweet and gentle guy, and he seemed so deep in thought. I just smiled at him and quickly leaned over and kissed him on the cheek, "Call me," I said as I shut the door and started for the house. I went inside and plopped on the couch, thinking it was a lovely weekend, but I was glad to be home now.

After that weekend, Brody and I spent a lot of time together, and it was nice to have someone to share things with in my life again. That summer, he came over and helped me plant the garden and work on the flowers in the yard. We became close friends, and we visited the girls more often, and they began coming for visits more often again. The fair came to town that summer, and Carrie came down with Mikayla, and we all went to the fair together. I took many pictures of Mikayla riding the ponies and eating cotton candy. Brody was good with Mikayla, and she started to call him Papa. He liked that a lot; it made him feel like he was part of a family again.

Brody's mother, Ella, was in the beginning stages of Alzheimer's disease. He had to move her into the nursing home, which greatly saddened him. Ella passed away that winter, and I helped Brody with all the funeral arrangements. It was sad because Brody was their only child, and now both of his parents were laid to rest. He felt like he didn't have anyone left. Brody never married and had no children, so after hanging out with him, we became his family. I still thought about Jesse often, and I had heard that he had moved out to Texas, but I made a point to walk away whenever I heard his name mentioned. I didn't want to know what he was doing or where he was. It was easier not knowing.

Brody and I became wonderful friends, and I knew he wanted to be more than that, but I could not offer anymore at that time. He seemed content with our friendship and didn't push me any further. There were times when we were out that he held my hand and tried to kiss me, but as soon as he felt me pull away, he stopped immediately and apologized. I knew I wasn't being fair to him, but it was all I could give right then.

For my 50th birthday, the girls planned a party with Brody and invited practically everyone from town. They had it up at the community center and hired a band and everything. I told them I didn't want them to go all out, and they didn't listen, of course. When I walked in, there were tons of decorations and balloons, the band played my favorite country music, and the whole town seemed to be there.

When I saw Maggie walk through the door, that was the best present I could have had. I ran to her with open arms. She looked frail and older, but she was still classy dressed, and her hair was all done up like Maggie always was. We all danced and laughed and had a wonderful time. Brody came and took my hand to dance a slow dance with me, and I was feeling some effects of the alcohol and stumbled into his arms. He caught me, and I giggled a bit, nuzzled into his arms, laid my head on his shoulder, and danced with him. "Thank you so much for this and all you are to me," I told him. "I would do anything for you, Kally," he whispered in my ear. I knew that Brody was in love with me, and I wanted to give him that kind of love back, but I couldn't bring myself to have those feelings again. It just hurt so much to go that route again, so I hardened my heart. I gave Brody as much as I could of myself, and that was all I could give.

Just then, I could hear the crowd change, I listened to the gasps and people chattering, and I turned to see what the commotion was, and there he was, coming across the room right towards me. He didn't stop to look at anyone else or care about what they were saying about him; he just kept walking right up to me with a fast pace and a grin on his face. My heart sank as I stepped back away from Brody and stood there with a dumb look on my face. My insides were spinning out of control, and I tried hard not to stumble. Still, he grabbed me up, hugged me tightly in a bear hug, and twirled me around, "Happy Birthday, Kal," he set me back down, and I swayed a bit with dizziness as he caught my arm. I didn't notice anyone else in the room; I just stared at Jesse, shocked to see him but still glad to see that he was okay.

"Jesse," I finally found the words to speak. "What are you doing here?" I asked. The music had stopped, and the crowd was silent, trying to catch the latest gossip. Some had smiles on their faces, some looking angry at the apparent hurt in Brody's eyes. Some shook their heads in disgust. I motioned for the band to continue playing, and I reached for Brody's hand and told them I had to sit down. Jesse followed behind us, and I heard him comment about Brody and me together, but I ignored it and kept walking to the table.

Jesse sat across from us at the table, giving Maggie a quick hug and telling her how nice it was to see her again. "I had to come back to wish Kal a happy birthday," he told her, acting as if everything was okay and pretending he could not feel the tension in the air. Cathy came rushing up to us at the table, and Jesse jumped to his feet as Cathy wrapped her arms around him, hugging him. "How the hell have you been, stranger," she said, trying to break the ice. "I've been okay, been living out in Corpus Christy, Texas. The kids are out there, and I have a grandson now," he told her, beaming with pride. He grabbed his wallet and showed us all pictures.

My heart had calmed down a bit, and still clutching onto Brody's hand, I looked at him to see his face wondering how he was doing with all of this. He leaned into me and whispered, "It is okay, Kally; I have learned to accept that you and Jesse will always share a connection. Have a fun birthday, honey, and don't worry about me" He squeezed my hand gently. I thought, "Wow, what an amazing guy" Just then, Jesse jumped up and grabbed my hand, "Dance with me, Kally," and before I could protest, he was dragging me out to the dance floor.

It was a slow song, and he wrapped his arms around me and held me as close as he could without crushing me. My body began to tingle, and I tried to push away gently but not make it too evident that his warm skin could still arouse me, and his smell made me dizzy. He put his hand on the back of my head, stroked my hair, and pushed lightly so that I laid my head on his shoulder.

"I missed you so much, Kally," he whispered. "Don't do this, Jesse, not now, never again," I sternly told him. "I know, it's just that I need you to know that I think about you all the time, and I will always miss you and love you," he whispered. A part of me wanted to run away with him, and the other part of me wanted to run away from him. "Brody isn't right for you," he said. Suddenly I became angry and pushed him back.

"You have no right, Jesse, to tell me who is right for me and who is not," I said louder than I expected to say. He grabbed my hand and pulled me to him again. "Shhhh, I am sorry" I know, you are right," he told me. "It's just that I can see that you are not in love with him," he whispered again. "Where is your girlfriend or your wife?" I smugly asked him. He then pointed towards the door. I looked over and saw the blonde woman I saw before standing by the doors, not looking too pleased but looking like she was patiently waiting for Jesse to get this out of his system again so he could go home with her. "She knows all about you, Kally, and she knows that she has to accept it if she wants to be in my life," he told me sadly. "Accept what"? I shouted.

The music stopped again, and the song was over, but we still stood in the middle of the floor, wrapped in each other's arms. Suddenly I realized that people were staring at us, and I pulled away from Jesse, embarrassed. "She has accepted that you are the only one that will ever have my heart, Kally" he leaned in and gently kissed me on my cheek. I touched my face where he had kissed me, and he told me to take care and walked towards the door. I wanted to run after him and have this out with him for the last time and demand him to stay the hell out of my life for good now, but I just stood there and watched him walk away.

Cathy came rushing to my side, "You okay? Come back to the table," she said, pulling my arm. I walked sadly back to the table and sat down next to Brody. He put his arm around my shoulder and gave me a quick squeeze, "are you okay?" he asked. "I am fine; let's dance," I told him. I grabbed my drink, chugged it down quickly, and told Maggie to order another one. She looked at me with concern but did as I asked. I danced and drank the night away and tried to forget about seeing Jesse. It did not work.

Soon I was a babbling drunk, and I told everyone how nice it was to see my good friend again. "He looked good, didn't you think? I asked Maggie. "Yes, he did," she agreed. They all could see right through me, and they knew how it was hurting me all over again to be without Jesse, so they just let me babble on. Soon Brody was clutching me, trying to hold me up, and told everyone that he was taking me home. Carrie and Jenni came to my side and kissed me, "Hope you had a good birthday, mamma," they told me. I smiled at them and kissed them both. "I had a wonderful birthday, my babies," I told them.

Brody helped me into the house, and he helped me get undressed and into bed. He sat on the edge of my bed then and asked if I was okay. I reached for his hand, held it in mine, and told Brody I was glad he was there. Then in a drunken state of mind, I went on to tell him that I was happy he was in my life and there for me over the years and what a wonderful man he truly was. I pulled him down towards me, and he lay beside me on the bed. I nuzzled in next to him, put my arms around him, and moved my hands under his shirt, caressing his belly and moving down toward the buttons on his jeans.

He grabbed my hand quickly, then stopped me. He rolled over on top of me, looking me in the eyes sternly, "Kally, I have wanted you to touch me for years now, and I have waited for this day, but I don't want you to do this when you are drunk and hurting because of seeing Jesse. It would be best if you didn't use me to stop your pain for one night of seeing Jesse walk out of your life again," he told me.

I didn't listen to him, and I continued to massage him and push my body closer to him seducing him. He pushed my hands away and tried to get up, but I put my arms around his neck, pulled him to me, and kissed him. He tried to pull away, but I wouldn't let him, and I wrapped my legs around him and pressed my body harder against him until I felt him respond. "Kally, are you sure about this?" He whispered. I continued rubbing his thighs and touching him until I could feel his body become aroused. "I know what you are doing, Kally, and you're going to feel awful in the morning, honey; I don't want our first time…." I grabbed him hard to me and kissed him harder and more aggressively so that he would stop talking.

I wanted to feel something again, and I didn't want him to analyze it to death. I rolled over on top of him then, and he gave in to my seduction, and we made love. I guess I wouldn't call it love because I wanted pure sex, which is what I got. I wasn't in love with Brody, and no matter how hard I tried to find those feelings, I just couldn't, so I settled for sex to get me through my broken heart of seeing Jesse again. The following morning, I woke up, and Brody was sleeping beside me. I slipped out of the room, trying not to wake him, and I went to put the coffee on in the kitchen. A few minutes later, Brody came out of the kitchen, came up behind me, and kissed me on the back of the neck. I moved away from him, and he knew then that it was only one night and nothing had changed between us. I could see the sadness in his eyes, and I felt terrible, but there was nothing I could do to change how I felt.

He made some excuse about having to be somewhere, and I was relieved to see him go. "I will call ya later, Kal," he said, and I smiled and said goodbye. I hated it when he called me Kal. Jesse always called me Kal, and I didn't like that Brody was trying to have that kind of relationship with me. I guess it was selfish of me to string Brody along like I was. Still, I liked having him as a friend whom I could go out and do things with, but I knew he had more feelings for me than I had for him, and it wasn't fair of me to keep leading him on. I was upfront with him and honest about my feelings, but still, it wasn't fair. I couldn't help but think about what happened with Joey and how guilty I still felt about the tragedy that occurred because of me.

Weeks passed, and I had yet to hear if Jesse had gone back to Texas or if he was still around, but I didn't ask anyone either. I went about my life, and when Cathy tried to bring the subject up on several occasions, I quickly steered her away from that subject. One day she just got furious with me and yelled, "I don't understand the two of you, it is obvious to everyone how much the two of you love each other, and it is clear to all of us that you both should be with each other, but yet you both are so stubborn."

I threw my hands up in the air and hollered back, "What would you like me to do about it? It is obvious that we can't get together no matter how hard I have tried to let him know how I feel, he doesn't trust it, or he doesn't feel the same way."

"Bullshit," she screamed. I stormed out of the room, yelling at her, "Conversation over, don't bring it up again! Jesse is not in my life, and he never will be," I told her. She gave up and left the office. She did not bring it up again to me.

Five years had passed since I saw Jesse last, and I had three more grandchildren. Jenni and Jim got married and had a baby of their own, a little girl, and they named her Jo, which was my middle name. Carrie gave birth to a set of twin boys; they named them Michael and James. James was Todd's middle name, and Michael was, of course, after her father. I was now a gramma of two granddaughters and two grandsons. Carrie and Todd moved back to town, and Todd got a job in the city and drove back and forth. I helped Carrie with the kids, and that spring, I had another hurdle to overcome.

I was at work when I got the phone call that informed me that Jenni was in a terrible car accident. I dropped the phone and ran out the door to rush to her side at the hospital. When I got to the hospital, they let me see her immediately. When I walked into her room, I gasped at the sight of my beautiful daughter and realized right then that it was more severe than I had thought. Her broken body was lying in the hospital bed with bandages covering her head, swollen eyes, and cuts and bruises. The tubes connecting her to many machines were more than my heart could handle. The tears came, and my body went weak as I knew my daughter was in for one hell of a fight ahead of her if she was going to survive this. Jim was standing in the hallway looking like a broken young man, and I asked him where Jo was. He told me in his shaking voice that she was with his mom in the waiting room.

They only let me stay in her room briefly, and when I came out of the room, Brody was standing there waiting to wrap me in his arms. I fell into his arms and sobbed hysterically. Shortly afterward, I heard the machines beeping, and doctors ran into Jenni's room and they rushed her into surgery. I only got to gently touch Jenni's hand as the doctors pushed the gurney swiftly past me. I watched Jim sink to the floor, sobbing. I called Carrie to tell her that she should come to the hospital. She said she would be there as soon as she could get a babysitter for the kids, and she showed up at the hospital an hour later. She came rushing over to me crying, and I held her as she sunk into my arms.

Jim's mom took Jo back to the house with the other kids and said she would help the babysitter with the kids. We waited for hours for word about Jenni and paced the hospital corridors. When I saw the doctor come down the hall towards us, I immediately saw the crushed look on his face. I knew instantly that he would tell me that Jenni didn't make it through the surgery. He reached out his hand to me as I fell to the floor by his feet, sobbing violently.

"I'm so sorry, Kally; we couldn't save her. There were too many internal injuries." The doctor explained. I pushed everyone who tried to console me away, and I jumped to my feet and ran out of the hospital. I didn't know where I was going; I just ran down the street. When I finally stopped, unable to catch my breath, I was at the park. I sat down on the bench, cried, and yelled at God for taking my child away. "How could you take her away from that sweet little girl?" I screamed out in pain. I was so angry and hurt I couldn't bare it. Jo needed her mommy, and God just took her away.

Losing a husband to death is extremely hard on the heart, but losing a child too soon is absolutely unbearable. It is not natural. A parent is supposed to die before their children. My phone was constantly ringing, and I ignored its ringing. I knew they were all looking for me, but I couldn't bear to talk to anyone. I just wanted to pretend for a moment that none of this was happening. I sat on the bench for hours with my head down, sobbing until I was too exhausted to move and too numb to feel anything. I jumped back, startled when a hand touched my shoulder, and I looked up, and there stood Jesse.

I burst into tears again, and he knelt beside me and cradled me in his arms. "Why is this happening, Jesse? It is not fair," I screamed out. He held and rocked me, "I know, baby, it's not fair," he agreed, caressed my hair, and kissed the top of my head, still holding me. "I can't go back there; please just get me out of here," I pleaded. He helped me to my feet, and we walked to his truck and got in. I laid on the front seat in his lap, and we drove off. We arrived at the hunting shack after driving a while, and Jesse had called the girls and told them that I was safe and that he would bring me home as soon as I could face things a little better.

I heard him on the phone tell Carrie that he was going to let me get some sleep and be alone for a while, and he would bring me home in the morning. "She is safe, and I will stay with her, Carrie. I know you need her, honey, but this has broken her right now, and she is no good to anyone now. Can you understand that?" he tried to explain to her. I could hear Carrie sobbing on the phone, and then Brody must have taken the phone because I heard Jesse's voice change. "She is with me, and I am taking care of her," he said sternly.

"I know that Carrie is a mess, but her mother needs time to pull things together before she can take care of anyone else. Can you understand that?" his voice raised a bit. "Just stay with Carrie and take care of her; I will bring Kally home as soon as she is able," he said, and he hung up the phone and came back over to me on the couch, sat on the floor beside the couch and put his arm around me rubbing my back as I sobbed into the pillow.

"Everything hurts, Jesse," I cried out. "My body hurts, and I am so angry" "Why is this happening?" I yelled and hit the pillow hard. Jesse grabbed my arms and held me close to his chest, and I cried hysterically, until I fell asleep exhausted. I awoke a couple of hours later, still dark out, screaming out as I dreamt of the horrible scene I had witnessed when I saw my child lying in that hospital bed, all battered and broken. I could not shake that picture out of my mind. Jesse wrapped his arms around me and held me close as I sobbed uncontrollably again.

I must have finally fallen asleep in Jesse's arms because the next thing I knew, the sun was shining in the window, and I heard birds chirping. I couldn't believe the sun could shine and the birds could still sing when my whole world felt torn apart. That made me angry too. I looked up, and Jesse was still cradling me tight in his arms, but his eyes were closed. I watched him for a while as he slept, and the tears kept rolling down my face. "How did Jesse find out so quickly, and how did he know where to find me when no one else could?" I thought to myself. He opened his eyes and caught me staring up at him, and he softly touched my cheek and wiped my tears away. He just continued to caress my face, not saying anything. His eyes had a deep concern for me, and I knew he wanted to take all my pain away from me, and it was killing him that he couldn't. He pulled me up to him and held me tightly as I began to sob again intensely. "Let me help you through this, Kally," he begged in a broken voice. I knew that he was feeling my pain as well.

Suddenly it dawned on me that I had to get home to my children. I had to get home to Jo. "Oh my God, Jesse, Jo needs me; we have to go" I jumped to my feet in a panic, and he grabbed me close to him. "Kally, I am not leaving you," he informed me sternly, and I looked up at his eyes and suddenly believed him with all my heart. I nodded my head and started for the door.

When we drove to the house, cars lined up in the driveway and down the block. All our friends were there from town helping my daughter through this and my grandchildren when I was not. Guilt took over me as I ran into the house with Jesse right behind me. Carrie sat on the couch with puffy eyes, and Brody was kneeling beside her, caressing her cheek and trying to console her. She saw me and immediately jumped up and ran into my arms, sobbing. I held her close, "I'm so sorry I ran out; I'm so sorry, Carrie, for leaving you," I wept.

There wasn't a dry eye in the room then, and the only thing I could think of is I wished they all would go home and leave us alone to mourn my beautiful baby girl. "Where is Jo?" I suddenly looked around the room for my granddaughter. "Cathy took her to your room to lay her down for a nap. She doesn't know what is going on, Mamma," Carrie said, still crying. I ran down the hall again, and Jesse followed me, not letting me too far out of his sight just in case I broke down again and needed him.

I entered the room and saw Cathy lying next to Jo on the bed, petting her golden curls as her eyes were fighting sleep. Her head popped up when she saw me come into the room "Gamma," she squealed in delight. I ran to her side, and Cathy immediately moved out of the way. I laid down next to Jo and held her close, trying not to let her see the tears rolling down my face. "This beautiful child would never know her wonderful, loving mother," I thought as I caressed her soft cheeks. Jo fell asleep then as I lay next to her. Jesse sat in the rocking chair next to my bed, and he reached out and held my hand as I fell asleep again.

The weeks ahead were excruciating. The friends I did not know I had, were there for me night and day, and it was amazing how a small town pulled together in a tragedy. I cannot thank everyone enough for getting me through the most challenging time of my life. The only thing that got me through it all was believing that Mike was right there to take our beautiful daughter's hand and take care of her from here on out until I could see her again. Her daddy would finally get to know her and be able to love her and take care of her. I was angry with God, but I still believed God would bring my little girl to her daddy.

I don't remember much about the funeral. I had sedatives to help me through it, I am ashamed to say, but that was my way of bearing a heavy load, and everything was just one big blur. Jim and his mom loaded my sweet granddaughter in the car, and we said our goodbyes. I begged Jim before he left to ensure that our sweet baby girl did not forget about our family. "Please, Jim, make sure she can visit us often," I pleaded. Jim promised me that he would not keep her from us. I gave him a hug, sobbing, and thanked him.

CHAPTER FIFTEEN

TRAGEDY BROUGHT US TOGETHER

Jesse was there for me through it all, and everyone was amazed that he had not left my side. There was talk around town that it wasn't fair of him to do this and then put me through another departure of his eventually, but I didn't care. I loved him for being by my side at this time, especially. Brody was hurting inside; I knew that. I knew he wanted to be the one there for me, but he settled for being there for Carrie and my grandbabies. He was a trooper through it all. He cooked and cleaned and took care of the babies as I shut myself away from the world in my room with Jesse next to me.

Carrie would come in and try and talk to me. I knew she wanted me to get up and move on with my life. Still, something inside me had just died, and I couldn't bring myself to look outside and see that the world didn't stop moving because my daughter was no longer with us. I only came out of my room to have a quick bite to eat and drink water and go back into my room. My body didn't seem to want to function anymore. I knew that Carrie was growing frustrated because she didn't know how to help me, and one day, she came into my room and snapped at me. She opened the curtains and let the sunshine in, yelling at me to get out of that bed. "You have grandbabies that want to hug their grandma, and you have another daughter that needs you, Mamma," she yelled and screamed hysterically, crying out.

I finally sat up in bed and looked at her sad, angry face. I remembered Ali doing the same thing when I decided to lock myself away after Mike had died. Then I looked at Jesse in the rocking chair, wondering if he felt the same way. Jesse nodded his head with a soft look in his eyes, letting me know that Carrie was right. "It's time Kal," he told me in a gentle, loving voice as he reached for my hand, and I forced my feet to the floor.

Jim returned a few weeks after the funeral and asked if Carrie would keep Jo for a while. He told her he wasn't suitable for her, and Carrie agreed to take her. It was hard to believe that three weeks had passed since the accident, and I decided to return to work again to try and get on with my life.

Carrie became Jo's second little mother and took care of her. Her daddy couldn't do it alone, but he was there for her every weekend when he didn't have to work. I was afraid that if I went back to work and got on with my life that Jesse would feel I didn't need him anymore, and he would leave my life again. I wasn't ready to let him go again, and I told him so. "I am not going anywhere, Kal," he said as he kissed my forehead gently. He told me he wasn't with his girlfriend anymore and was moving back home to be closer to me. "I want you and I to make this work, and It is time that we both stay where we belong, together," he told me. I wrapped my arms around his neck and kissed him passionately.

My first day back to work was difficult, but I managed to make it until 3 pm, and then I told them I had to go home. They all understood and seemed amazed that I made it almost all day. I got home, and instead of crawling into my bed, I decided to go into the kitchen and make cookies. I called Carrie and told her to bring the kids and come over for supper, and she agreed excitedly. I contacted Jesse and asked him to be here at 6 for supper, and he said he would.

I prepared meatloaf and mashed potatoes, and around 5 pm, I heard the front door open. I expected it to be Carrie with the kids arriving early, but Brody walked into the kitchen.

"I need to talk to you, Kally," he told me with sadness in his eyes. I quickly sat down at the table and let him speak. He told me that he waited a long time for me to get over Jesse and fall in love with him, but deep down, Brody always knew that he would never have that place in my heart. "I hoped it would happen one day, but I always knew that Jesse held that place in your heart, and I guess I should have listened to the whole town tell me that it was never going to happen," he spoke. "I am happy for you and Jesse; I sincerely am, and I hope it works out for the two of you." He stood up next to me and reached for my hand. I sat there, letting him hold my hand, and I listened to him continue.

"I love you, Kally, with all my heart, and that is why I have to say goodbye to you. My heart cannot stand seeing you with another man no matter how much I told myself that this was going to happen," he told me. "I have to walk away and let you stand on your own two feet and be happy" I stood up then and hugged him close. "Brody, you have been wonderful to my girls and me and have been there for us for so many years that I don't know what I would have done without you. You were my rock for so long, and I am sorry I hurt you," I told him.

He held his finger to my lips and shushed me, "You have never led me to believe that you were anything more than a great friend to me, honey" You didn't hurt me at all. I am the one that fell in love with you, and I am the one that let myself believe that you would come around someday and give me the same feelings back. You always told me that we were just friends, and you always made it perfectly clear to me who had your heart all along". He kissed my forehead then and told me he wished me all the happiness in the world, and he turned and left. Tears rolled down my cheeks as I thought about what a kind and loving friend Brody had been to me all these years, and it made me sad to think that things were going to drastically change between us now that Jesse was back. I quickly wiped the tears from my eyes as I heard the front door slam and Carrie's voice call out, "Mom, you home?"

"In here," I shouted back. Carrie came into the kitchen and hugged me. "Where are the kids?" I asked. She told me that Todd was picking them up from the sitter after work, and she just wanted to come and help me make dinner and have some alone time with me. "Oh," I said with my eyebrows raised. Knowing full well that it meant she would discuss Jesse with me. "Mom, we need to talk about your decision with Jesse" "I knew it," I put my hand up to her in protest.

"It is my decision Carrie, and I am a big girl," I told her. "I know, and it is no surprise to any of us that you would choose this decision, but we also know what it does to you when Jesse walks away and leaves you empty again and again. We don't want to see you hurt again." Her eyes were welling up with tears as she spoke. I gave her a quick hug with tears in my eyes and told her that I knew what I was doing even though I had no idea what Jesse and I were doing.

I was terrified to open my heart up again, but I couldn't tell Carrie that. I was scared of a broken heart, but I was more afraid of never knowing what our lives would be like if Jesse and I didn't try to make things work between us. I didn't want to go to my heavenly maker, not knowing why Jesse and I didn't grow old together. It was evident that there was this lasting connection between us, and no matter how many times each of us has tried to walk away from it and move on with our lives, neither of us ever could. "It's going to be okay, Carrie," I tried to reassure her, not showing the doubt in my heart. "Now help me with supper; everyone will be here soon," I demanded. Carrie tried to stay in the conversation, but I shushed her immediately, and she reluctantly gave up and started setting the table.

We had a nice dinner, and the kids all chattered, and the house was, by all means, not peaceful, but it was very nice to see some normal behavior in all of us. Looking at Jo sitting in her high chair, I saw Jenni in her so much. I fought back the tears when I thought this child would never know what a beautiful mother she once had. Jesse put his hand on my thigh and caressed me gently. I looked at him and nodded, letting him know I was okay. After dinner, we all pitched in to clean things up, and Todd took the kids into the living room to play. It was a good evening, but I was exhausted. It was nice when everyone went home, and Jesse and I spent the rest of the evening alone.

I lay on the couch as Jesse put in a movie for us to watch, and he came and sat down on the sofa, lifting my head gently and setting it in his lap. I lay there looking up at him as he stroked my cheek and moved the hair away from my face as he always did. "I love you, Kally," he told me. I smiled, said, "Back at ya," closed my eyes, and drifted off to sleep. I woke up hours later and looked at the clock on the wall. It was 2 am, and I looked up at Jesse, still in the same position with his eyes closed, making cute little snoring noises.

It looked like neither one of us had watched the movie. I smiled and reached to touch his cheek, and he opened his eyes and looked down at me, and responded by running his fingers through my hair gently and then moving his hand down the middle of my back, pressing my body closer to him. I sat up and moved in closer to him, and he put both hands on my face pulling me into him and kissing me passionately; without a second to spare, he rolled me to my back and moved on top of me, kissing my neck and moving his hands down my body caressing my inner thighs as I responded emotionally.

He moved his mouth down to my breast and started peeling off my shirt and baring my breasts so he could suck each nipple and send arousing chills throughout my body. My legs began to shake, and my heart was pounding as I moved my body into him closer. He unbuckled my belt, unzipped my pants, and his hand moved inside my jeans, and in no time, I was lying underneath him naked and warm with his body on top of me, kissing my belly and his tongue, exploring every inch of my body. Jesse was then on top of me, and his naked body was pushing against me tightly. He inserted himself inside me harder and harder, and our bodies were one.

Making love to Jesse was the only thing in my life that made sense then, and I didn't want it ever to stop. We made love until the morning sun was shining through the window, and both extremely tired, we fell asleep in each other's arms. When we woke again, it was already 10 am, and I got up to shower. Jesse grabbed my arm as I was getting up. "Where are you going? I'm not finished with you yet," he teased. I smiled and quickly kissed him, and he took my hand and kissed my fingers one at a time.

"Marry me, Kally" I shook my head at him and laughed; he grabbed my hand again and pulled me down on the couch next to him. With a serious look on his face, he said again, "Marry me, Kally" I put my hand on his chest and slightly pushed him away from me. "Not yet, Jesse, it's too soon for us," I told him. His face looked hurt, like a child that just got scolded, and I quickly wrapped my arms around him and tried to explain. I told him I wanted us to be together for the rest of our lives. Still, after all these years of not knowing where he was or what kept us apart for so long, I wanted to be able to trust that he was going to stick around from now on, and it wasn't just because things were so emotional for me and that he felt sorry for me right now.

Jesse grabbed me, held me tight, and assured me he was there because he wanted to be there, but he understood where I was coming from and why I was concerned. "I will keep asking you, Kally, until you say yes" he smiled at me and kissed my forehead. I smiled back and got up to take a shower.

In the months that followed, Jesse kept his word, he asked me to marry him on several occasions, and I just kept smiling and shaking my head, "Not yet, baby," I kept telling him. It became a game for both of us. I couldn't have been any happier, though, spending time with him again and having him to lean on. He was my second chance at true love, and I knew in my heart that we were supposed to be together. Carrie and Jesse became close, and she began to trust that he was going to stick around this time, so of course, he had her on his side, and she was urging me to say yes. "What are you waiting for, mamma?" she asked one day when she and the kids came to visit. I smiled and changed the subject; she shook her head in frustration.

Life was going well then, and even though I missed Jenni every day, I was still happy to wake up with Jesse's arms around me and kiss him goodbye every morning as we both went to work. It was one of the highlights of my days; the other highlight was kissing him again when we both came home from work. We had wasted many years pushing each other away because neither of us felt we deserved to be happy. I realized that Mike would have wanted me to be happy and in love again, and he would have done anything to ensure our girls had a great life.

It comforts me that Jenni is united again with her daddy, and Mike is at peace taking care of her. I only wish that Jesse truly believed he deserved happiness as well. Jesse had a hard time forgiving himself for all the pain that he felt he caused in our lives.

Jesse also could not forgive himself for taking the life of another person. He had many nightmares but never wanted to discuss them with me.

Sometimes he would wake up in a cold sweat, and his body shook. I tried to console him, but he brushed me away and got out of bed. He would go downstairs, and I would find him on the couch the next morning. I asked him to talk to a professional, and he snapped at me, "I'm not crazy. I told him that I did not think he was crazy; I just felt that he needed to talk to someone that could help him learn how to forgive himself.

He constantly changed the subject and brushed me off when it came to that subject. Most of the time, I just let it go because I was incredibly happy that we finally found a place in our relationship that didn't involve running away from each other. That winter, Jesse moved in with me. We both decided to stay in Springfield, where all our friends were. Jesse's girls were a plane ride away to visit, and Carrie and Todd and my beautiful grandkids were back in Springfield, and Jo was living with Carrie and Todd right now, but even if she went back home, she would only be a couple of hours away.

Jesse got his old job working with heating and air conditioning, and everything seemed peaceful in our lives. Well, you know what they say about the calm before the storm, don't you? It was about to come crashing in like a title wave.

CHAPTER SIXTEEN

SECRETS OF THE PAST

I took the day off from work to prepare for our annual garage sale fundraiser for the Springfield Jaycees, and I was going through some boxes in the garage when I came across the old cardboard box with Mike's belongings in it. I had forgotten all about it and was too broken back then to even look at its contents. I slowly peeled the tape back and opened the box. I pulled out his military uniform and hat. It was nicely pressed and still looked brand new. There was a pack of cigars and a lighter. I remember Mike used to enjoy a cigar occasionally when he got together with the guys for a drink. I pulled out a small container and opened it, and it had a key in it with a piece of paper with some numbers written on it.

There were some shoes, an autographed baseball from someone that I could not make out the writing, and Mike's old thermos that he used to take in the car on long trips. In the corner of the box was an envelope with some paperwork inside and pictures. I pulled out the contents, and the paperwork was a deed to some property out in California. I had never seen it before and wondered when Mike had purchased this property. His name was on the document, but I had never heard anything about it. I glanced at the pictures briefly but then pulled out the letter inside the envelope.

The letter read:

Dear Michael,

I know you do not understand why I left you with your gramma Ali, but I wanted you to know that I loved you from the first time I laid eyes on you until my last breath. I had many troubles growing up, and most were definitely my fault, but there are things that I need you to know before it is too late. I don't want my secrets to go into the ground with me. I have a terminal illness, and I wanted to say goodbye. You have a brother, and I want you to find him and get to know him. He is terrific, and the two of you would be great friends.

It's essential to have someone in your life to love always. I was never able to take care of myself, let alone children, so he went to live with friends of mine, and they raised him as their own. His name is Jesse, and he grew up in Springfield, Wisconsin. I wanted you both to know that I always checked in on you, even though your Gramma Ali would never let me talk to you. I cared, and I asked about you. I am in a hospital right now, and they are taking care of me, and it is any day now that I will be checking out of this world. I love you, and I am proud of whom you have become. You are a fine young man. Hope to see you on the other side.

Love your Mamma

I gasped as I read the words brother, and his name is Jesse. He lives in Springfield, Wisconsin. Is this a coincidence? A bad joke? I thought to myself. I kept digging through the box, trying to find more answers, but there was nothing else. I suddenly remembered the key and wondered if there might be more answers to whatever that key opened. It looked like a key to a safe deposit box, so I quickly put everything back in the box and tucked it under the garage shelf. I ran into the house and looked up the number of the bank that Mike used to bank at out in California. I picked up the phone and called. "Good morning, First National Bank.

This is Sharon. Can I help you?" The woman on the phone asked. "Yes, do you have a safe deposit box with the number 265983218?" I asked. "One moment as I look it up, please." She replied. Within seconds she returned to the line and told me, yes, Mike Kalhoun occupied that box. I asked her if someone was paying the monthly bill, and she said yes. I was confused and tried to pry further, but she suddenly became suspicious, would not tell me anything else, and told me to have a nice day.

I wondered who was paying the safe deposit box bill each month. Ali had passed away; it couldn't be her paying the bill, I thought, but what about Maggie? I called Maggie, and there was no answer, so I left a message that she needed to call me back as soon as she got this message. I sunk into my chair, and the wheels in my head were turning so quickly. I wondered if Jesse could be Mike's long-lost brother, and if so, did he know about Mike? Did he know it was my Mike? All these emotions were winding up inside of me, and I needed to know the truth, but where was I to begin? My thoughts were interrupted by the slamming of the front door.

"Hey Kal, you home?" Jesse's voice rang out. I shoved the key and the note with the numbers on it into my pocket and quickly walked into the kitchen, where Jesse was standing in the open refrigerator. "Are you hungry? I can start some lunch for you," I offered. "No, I am just going to grab a quick sandwich, and then I am going over to the garage to fix my tire. As I was going around the creek corner, my tire blew out," He griped. "Oh, good thing you are okay," I told him. Jesse kissed me on the forehead and said, "You always look at the bright side of things, Kal! I love that about you." He smiled.

"Jesse, can we go for supper tonight and talk?" I asked. "Sure thing, I should be home around 6," he replied. I smiled, and he hugged me quickly as he darted out the door. "Love ya, Kal," Jesse winked and hollered back, "You will marry me soon!" I smiled and waved goodbye. As I closed the door, the phone rang, and I ran to pick it up.

It was Maggie. "Kally, what's wrong?" She sounded frantic. "No, Maggie, everything is fine; sorry to make you worry," I reassured her. "I just have some questions, and it is going to sound like I am crazy," I told her. I explained to her that I had found this key, a safe deposit box out in California at the bank where Mike used to do his banking. Maggie got quiet on the phone. "Do you know about this?" I asked. There was silence for a while, and I said, "Please, Maggie, if you know something." I heard her breathe deeply and sigh, and then she began.

She told me that Mike had received a letter from his mother years ago and that she told him that she was in hospice and didn't have very much longer to live. Mike didn't want Ali to know any of this because it would have made her sad. Ali constantly worried about her daughter, but it gave her great comfort just believing she was out there and living her life. It would have hurt her badly if she knew her daughter had died.

"So, Mike locked up the secrets in a safe deposit box," Maggie told me. Maggie said Mike didn't want those secrets out for Ali to be hurt by any of it, so she continued to pay the safe deposit fee for him after he had died. "I have no clue what is in that box, Kally; I just paid the fee," Maggie assured me. I told Maggie that in the letter, Evie said she tried to reach out to Mike, but Ali wouldn't allow it. Maggie said it was true that Evie reached out, but every time, she was using drugs and alcohol, and that is why Ali refused her visits until one day, she stopped asking. I told her I had to know everything, and now that Ali had passed away, I felt those secrets needed to come out. She understood and offered to make the trip with me. I told her I would let her know, and we said goodbye and hung up the phone.

That night at dinner, I was quiet, and Jesse asked what was going on with me. I told him that as I was going through some boxes in the garage, I came across an old property deed that Mike had tucked away in a box, and I needed to take a trip out to California to investigate this deed. It was not a lie. I did need to investigate that as well. I had to find out where this property was, and I knew that all my answers to my questions were back in Newbury Springs, California, so that is where I needed to go. Jesse knew he wouldn't change my mind, so he offered to go with me. I told him that I needed to do this alone.

"Please understand, Jesse, I won't be gone long, I promise," I said. He reluctantly agreed. I also tried to pry some information out of him by asking him what he remembers about his parents. He told me they were good people, and he recalled that his dad worked a lot, but his mother was always home taking care of him and his sister. His Sister Sherri was quite a bit older than him, and they didn't look like each other. She had blonde hair and blue eyes and looked a lot like his mom, he told me.

"I guess I looked like my dad," he shrugged. I asked if he ever had a brother, and he darted a confused look at me and said, "No, Kally, I told you, I only have one sister" "Oh yes, that's right, I remember," I stuttered awkwardly. He suddenly grew suspicious and asked, "What's with all the questions all of a sudden, Kally" "No reason, I just like to know everything about you," I lied. We finished our dinner as it was getting late, and Jesse had to work early in the morning on a big job they were doing outside of town. I decided to wait to tell Jesse about the letter I had found until I could find out more information.

That night as we lay next to each other in bed, Jesse reached over and touched my arm gently, and his hand began to move down my back, exploring for a response from me. It was hard not to respond, but I couldn't shake the feeling that Jesse might be Mike's brother, and it bothered me to no end not knowing if the two of them knew about each other. In the letter, his mom had said that she reached out to both of her boys, so Jesse would have had to receive something from her, too, right? I couldn't shut my thoughts off, and Jesse finally sat up in bed and, in an obviously frustrated voice, said, "Kally, what the hell is going on with you?" "I'm sorry Jesse, it's just that going through Mike's old things brought so many memories back and ghosts; I am just a little shaken today," I told him with tears in my eyes. Jesse reached over and cuddled me in close, kissed my forehead, and we both fell asleep.

The next morning, I got up to have coffee with Jesse before he went to work. I told him that I would book my flight and hotel and rent a car when I arrived in California. He kissed me goodbye and told me to be careful and keep in touch with him. I assured him that I would. After Jesse left, I began planning my trip. The earliest flight out was 3 pm, so I packed and prepared for my trip. I decided I needed to do this alone, and I left Maggie a message on her voicemail letting her know. I safely tucked the key and note into my purse and ran out to the garage to get the deed, the letter, pictures, and a few other papers in the envelope. I wanted to look at the photographs when I was on the plane. I arrived at the airport, parked my car in the underground garage, grabbed my luggage, and rushed to check in. By 3:10 pm, I was in the air.

Immediately upon landing, I went to get my luggage and walked to the other side of the airport to rent a car. I chose a red Chevy Equinox that was clean and shiny, and I started it up and headed for my hotel. I checked into my hotel and had about a 45-minute drive to Newberry Springs, but the bank's location was in Barstow, so that would be my first stop. When I arrived, I walked into the small bank, walked up to the teller, and told her I needed to check my safe deposit box. She asked me what number, and I told her. A security guard escorted me to the safe deposit box room and directed me into the secure room that he pointed at where I could have some privacy. I found the box and put the key in and turned it.

My whole body began to tremble, and suddenly I felt panicked about not knowing what I would find. I removed the box, walked to the small, private room, and closed the door. I also felt like I was doing something illegal, which scared me. I stood there staring at the unopened box, took a few deep breaths, and opened the box up. I was shocked to see large amounts of cash bundled in 3 large stacks. I removed the money and set it on the table. Under the cash were photographs of a woman with an infant child. The woman was beautiful, with long, black, wavy curls flowing down.

She was sitting on the porch swing I had recognized at Ali's house. I also realized it was Evie from the pictures I had seen at Ali's home.

The infant child in her arms must be Mike. There was another picture underneath, and as I looked at it, I saw that it was Evie again, but she looked older and sad in this photo. She held the hand of a small young boy with big dark brown eyes and messy brown hair. His shirt was tattered and torn, and he looked like he was also sad. Tears fell down my eyes looking at this photo. I turned the picture over, and there was writing on the back that said Mamma and Jesse, age 3, and in parenthesis, it noted (Find him, Michael, he needs you). I gasped for air and began to cry. "What did this all mean" I questioned.

I had to find out more information before I could go to Jesse with this. I had brought a bag with me to put the contents of the box in, and I continued to unload the safety deposit box in my bag and zipped it shut. There were a few more papers in an envelope that I didn't look at and some jewelry. I put the deposit box back in place and carried my bag to the teller's window. I informed her that I wanted to close the safety deposit box so they would stop the billing. I had to show her Mike's death certificate to close the account. I left the bank and drove to Newberry Springs. I pulled into the parking lot at the Shanty Inn and locked the bag in the car's trunk.

I walked into the bar and didn't recognize anyone in the place. Josh must have parted ways here, and new owners were behind the bar. I had one drink and left. I hoped to see Josh and tell him I was doing okay and catch up as old friends do. I had left in such a hurry years ago, and it would have been nice to see how he was doing.

I wondered where all this cash had come from and if Mike may have been into something illegal. Back at the hotel, I went through the paperwork that I had found, and I couldn't make heads or tails of any of it, so I decided that I probably should talk to a lawyer about the deed that I had found and the paperwork that looked like legal paperwork as well. I only stayed one night, and the following day I boarded a flight back home, still not knowing all the facts about what I had found.

When I arrived back home, Jesse's truck was in the driveway. I still did not have enough facts to bring this information to him, so I decided to keep it to myself and search for more truth. I couldn't help but think that Maggie knew more than she was letting on, so I started planning my next trip to see her. I told Jesse that I wanted to go out and visit Maggie for a couple of days, and he thought that was a great idea, so I took a few days off from work and started my journey early in the morning. I decided to surprise her, and I called her when I was only a few miles from her place to make sure she was home.

"Hi, Kally," she answered. "Hey Maggie, I was wondering if you were around so I could stop over and say hello. I am only a few minutes away," I told her. She was excited to see me, but in her voice, I could hear reluctance. When I arrived, she had coffee on and invited me. I grabbed my suitcase from the car and hugged her as I entered. "How long are you planning on staying, Kally?" Maggie asked. I told her a couple of days and that I could get a hotel nearby if that would be more convenient. "Nonsense! You will stay right here with me," she insisted. That night over supper, we talked and talked about little things. It was nice to catch up on each other's lives and the small happenings we both encountered daily. It was good to see Maggie again, and it felt great to relax and get away. We talked about Ali and how much we both missed her but agreed that she was in a better place.

After a while, we finally broke the ice when she asked how my trip to California went. I told her that I didn't find much information, but I told her about the large amount of cash in the safe deposit box and that I found two property deeds. I also told her about the photos that I found. She put her head down and patted her eyes with a tissue, and I could tell she was agitated. "Maggie, tell me what you know, please," I begged her. Tears welled up in her eyes, and she took a deep breath. "Okay," she said. "I will tell you everything that I know," she assured.

She told me that Mike received a letter from Evie when he was 20 years old and had just enlisted in the service. It was the letter that I had found in his belongings. She started sending him money in the mail, and he kept putting it away, never spending it because he was sure it was dirty money and wanted nothing to do with it. He never wrote back to Evie because he didn't want to be involved in anything that had anything to do with Evie. "Mike never believed that Evie was dying,"

Maggie said. "He only thought that was her way to slither back into his life ." She told me. Maggie said that Mike was always curious about Jesse, and he hired a private investigator to find him. He wasn't sure that Jesse existed or if he was his half-brother because he didn't believe a word Evie said, but his curiosity forced him to search until he found him.

Jesse was about 15 years old then, and he went and saw him at his high school playing football. Mike watched him with his friends and said Jesse looked like a great football player. Mike told Maggie that Jesse looked like he was fine and well-adjusted. Mike told her he was just about to approach him after practice was over, but he stopped when he saw Jesse walk up to a woman who looked a lot like Evie. "Mike got in his car and left immediately," Maggie said. "He thought maybe the two were up to something together, and he didn't trust the situation." Maggie had tears in her eyes. "There is more, isn't there?" I asked.

Maggie nodded her head and continued. She told me that Mike and she were not related. Maggie said she used to babysit for Mike when he was two years old, and she was 12 years old and lived next door. Maggie told me that her parents died in a terrible car crash when she was 14 years old, and she had no other relatives to take her in, so Ali fought for her, took her in, and raised her.

She told me that the two properties are in California. "Those properties are connected, and that was going to be an anniversary present from Mike to you and the girls the year Mike passed away." She was crying then. "I didn't have the heart to tell you, and when you chose to pick a new place and create your brand-new start, I just let you go and buried it," she cried. "I am so sorry, Kally; I never meant to hurt you in any way," she vowed. I cried hysterically, asking her why she wouldn't tell me about Jesse. She told me that when I came up to say goodbye to Ali, and I introduced her to Jesse, she knew he was Mike's brother as soon as she looked at his face. "I looked in his eyes and saw that warm smile, and I just knew," she sobbed.

"When you told us that you were moving to Springfield, Wisconsin, I couldn't believe my ears," she told me. "I told myself it was Mike guiding you there, so I said nothing, and I am truly sorry," she cried.

Maggie told me the cash envelopes stopped coming after Mike turned 27. She believed it was because Evie died, but Mike still didn't think that, and shortly after that, Mike passed away, so she never found out if Evie was still alive or had died. She believes Jesse would know that information if Evie stayed in touch with him, but she doesn't think Jesse ever knew about Mike.

I stayed with Maggie for a couple of days, and we hashed everything over, trying to figure out what the missing puzzle pieces were. Still, the only way I was ever going to find out everything is bringing Jesse in on everything and finding out what happened to Evie. I started on my journey home that morning, and a thousand thoughts were going through my head. How would I even begin to open this whole can of worms to Jesse, and how would he even take it? It scared me to death. Jesse is known to pack up and run off when he feels things are too heavy to handle. I was so afraid of losing him all over again. It was about 2 pm when I arrived home, and Jesse's truck was in the driveway. It was a Saturday, and he finally got a weekend off. He was excited to hang out at home and complete some much-needed tasks around the house that he had been putting off.

I walked in the door with my suitcase, and he immediately got up from the couch to come and help me carry my bags to the bedroom. "Hey honey, did you have a nice trip?" he asked, patting me on my backside and kissing my cheek. I told him yes, it was nice to see Maggie again and I started unpacking my suitcase. "You okay, babe"? He questioned. I yawned and told him I was tired from the long drive. "I'm going to take a hot shower and lie down for a while," I told him. He reached out his arms and hugged me, kissed my forehead, and told me to get some rest.

Jesse was such a giving and kind man, but he was also fragile. I was so worried that I was going to be the one that was going to bring turmoil to his life again.

That night at dinner, I told Jesse that I needed to talk to him about some important things I had found in Mike's belongings. I told him I had forgotten all about the box I had stashed away in the basement years ago. Jesse looked at me, puzzled, and probably wondered what it had to do with him.

I then told him that Mike's mother's name was Evie, and she had left him with his grandmother, Ali, when he was only eight months old. I looked at Jesse to see if his reaction had changed, but he continued to look at me attentively. I then told him that I found a letter in the box and would like him to read it. Jesse took the letter and began reading it, and after a couple of minutes, I could tell by the look on his face that he knew where this was all leading.

When he finished reading the letter, he looked up at me, and tears were in his eyes. "So, you think Evie is my mother?" he asked in a soft, broken voice. I then gave him the photograph. I told him everything about the safety deposit box, the money, the deeds, the photos, and the letters I had found. I asked him if he had ever remembered meeting the woman in the photograph, and he didn't think so, but it was such a long time ago. He told me that it was time that we both talked to his sister to find out if she knew anything.

The following day Jesse called Sherri and asked if we could all meet for a cup of coffee. She was surprised that Jesse had invited her but quickly agreed. We arrived at 10 am to avoid the morning and lunch crowd. Jesse didn't waste any time asking Sherri if he was adopted. The look on her face was utter shock and a dead giveaway that she knew more information than we did. "I need to know everything," he demanded quietly. Sherri took a deep breath and began her story.

She told us that Jesse's biological mother was into drugs and partying. "She used to work with our mother years ago," she spoke.

"Our mom was babysitting you one night, and Evelyn never returned," Sherri told us that her mother tried getting a hold of Evie, but her phone was no longer in service. She didn't want Jesse to enter the system, so Sherri's parents decided to raise Jesse as their child, at least until Evie returned. Sherri said that she was old enough to know what had happened and that her parents had asked her if she wanted a brother, and she agreed. They also told her that it had to be a secret and Jesse would be raised as their child. She said Jesse was just a baby when Evie left him, but she did come back for two days, but it was only to ask for money.

"Mom saw Evie's tattered clothing and uncombed hair, and she wreaked of alcohol, so mom gave her money only after she threatened to take Jesse away." "She knew Jesse didn't stand a chance in life if he was with his mother. Sherri pointed to the picture we had shown her and confirmed that this was when she returned. Sherri said that Evie had taken the picture with her so she could remember Jesse, and then she left and never returned.

"How did you find all this out, Jesse?" Sherri asked. Jesse told her the whole story about the box in my basement belonging to my husband, Mike. He told her the entire story. She was shocked to hear that Jesse had a brother and equally shocked to learn it was my husband that passed away so tragically years ago. "Wow, unbelievable!" Sherri shrieked. "What an amazing story, and how truly inspirational! It isn't chance that the two of you met; it was fate!" Sherri exclaimed with tears in her eyes. Jesse put his arm around me and nudged me close to him.

I asked Jesse if he remembered meeting the woman in the photo when he was older. Talking about everything did jog his memory, and Jesse vaguely remembered meeting a woman at his football practice that called him over to the fence. It was a few days after his parents had passed away. The woman told him that she was sorry for the loss of his parents and asked if he would be okay. "I remember asking her if she knew my parents, and she told me she was good friends with my mom," he said. "I remember telling her that Sherri and I were living with Grandpa and Grandma on the farm." He remembers feeling weird about talking to her, but he told her that his grandparents were taking care of everything. The woman smiled and told him, "God Bless," as she turned and walked away.

He never knew until now that the woman was his biological mother, Evie. She wasn't fit to be a mother to both Mike and Jesse, but that didn't mean that her heart didn't ache for them and she didn't care about their well-being. We all sat in silence, pondering on everything we had learned.

That night we lay in bed holding each other and drifted off to sleep in peace. The following morning over a cup of coffee, I told Jesse that we would have to explain all of this to the family. We decided to plan a dinner party and invite the whole family. We agreed on the following Saturday, and I called Carrie to see if her family would be available to attend. She was happy to hear from me and told me she was just about to call me.

"I have news, and you might want to sit down," she requested. My heart sank a bit, not knowing what she was about to tell me and not knowing if I could take any more mysterious news. "What is it?" I asked. "Jim called me last week to talk about Jo," Carrie replied. Carrie told me that Jim could not get over the loss of Jenni, and every time he looked at Jo, it was painful for him. Jim told Carrie that he couldn't raise Jo the way Jenni would want her raised, and he begged Carrie to take her and make her life fantastic and full of love. He told Carrie that Jenni would have wanted Jo to have a mother like Carrie if Jenni wasn't able to be there for her. "I talked to Todd, and we decided to take Jo," Carrie announced.

"Oh, Carrie! That is wonderful but so sad for Jim," I responded. I asked her if Jim had planned on staying in Jo's life, and Carrie told me that he promised if time healed his wounds, he would reach out to Jo, but he didn't want to be her full-time father. Carrie agreed to come next Saturday for dinner, and we hung up the phone.

I sat at the kitchen table and thought about how sad Jim must be to make that decision. I saw his face when that beautiful child came into the world. It was the face of a proud daddy that had more love to give this little girl than anyone. Everyone grieves in different ways, I thought to myself. On a happy note, I know Jo will be close to our family and have a good life.

CHAPTER SEVENTEEN

TOGETHER AT LAST

The Friday before our family dinner, I prepared salads and prepared for our meal. Jesse helped with the household chores, and we were excited to see everyone. Jesse's girls were flying in that night, and Jesse had to pick them up at the airport at 9 pm. I hadn't seen his girls in such a long time. They both had finished college, and Jessica was still living out in Texas, but Bella had moved to Florida with some college friends she had met.

Bella was an RN at a University hospital and was still single. Jessica was a CPA accountant at a Texas tax office. She was dating and living with a man she had met in college. His name was Bryce. They had two boys, ages 2 and 3 years old. Sam and Cory were their names. The last time I saw them both, they were in their pre-teens. I was nervous to see them and hoped that they still remembered me. Jesse left for the airport, and I quickly jumped into the shower to prepare for their arrival.

When they arrived, I came down wearing jeans and a loose-fit pink top with sparkles. I curled my hair and put a small amount of makeup on. Both girls hugged me and said hello, and I couldn't believe how grown-up they both looked. Time sure flew by. They were both gorgeous girls and extremely polite. I showed them their rooms where they would be staying, and they both went to take their suitcases to their temporary living quarters. I asked where the kids were, and Jessica told me that Bryce was on daddy duty for the weekend. I went to the kitchen and made a small snack for everyone, as I figured they might be hungry after their travels.

We all watched a movie that night and snacked on some popcorn. The girls caught us up on their life's activities, and we were glad they seemed happy and well-grounded.

The following day, we had a light breakfast together, cleaned up the house, and got ready for the rest of our guests to arrive. By 1 pm, everyone was mingling and getting to know each other. The kids were running around the house, playing, giggling, and having a blast. It was nice to have everyone together. I had a roast in the oven and potatoes on the stove simmering. Jesse had asked if I wanted to make our announcement before dinner, and I agreed. We called everyone to the living room and began our story, letting everyone know all the details we had discovered about our families. Everyone seemed to take it very well, but they were stunned at the news. After discussing and asking questions, Carrie shouted, "It is fate," and everyone agreed that miracles brought Jesse and me together.

At that moment, Jesse reached for both my hands and stood in front of me. I looked at him, smiling a sheepish grin, and he suddenly got down on one knee and held open a ring box with a beautiful ring inside. "Kally, we have gone through so many years of heartache, happiness, tragedy, and many difficult obstacles. Through it all, I have loved you every second of every day, and I don't want to spend another second without you by my side. Please Marry me and be my best friend and wife for the rest of our days on this earth." he spoke with tears in his eyes.

The house was so quiet you could hear a pin drop. It seemed like everyone was holding their breath until they heard me shout the word. "YES," I wrapped my arms around him and kissed his tender lips sweetly. Then the house chimed with hooting, hollering, and clapping in approval of our whole family. I heard yelling, "Finally!" come from Carrie, and she ran over to hug us both.

When we had the house back to ourselves, we began making plans for a small but beautiful wedding day. We decided we didn't want to wait, so we planned to marry in the summer. We prepared a June wedding and invited family and a small group of friends. We also decided that we wanted the wedding to be in the backyard and a reception and dance afterward. A backyard BBQ was our choice.

Jesse and I decided to take the money in that safe deposit box and split it between all our children and grandchildren. The total came to $135,000, and we weren't quite sure if it was drug money or how Evie came across that kind of cash, so we discussed it with a lawyer and figured out a way to make it legal but pay the least amount of taxes on it. The kids were thrilled. Jesse also dug for information on what happened to Evie. He discovered she was telling the truth about being sick; she just lived longer than expected. She passed away shortly after her visit to see Jesse when he was 15 years old and was buried in Colorado. Jesse wasn't sure if she had a funeral or anything, but the state took care of the burial. That made Jesse very sad that no one could help her straighten out her life. Many people tried to be there for her, but her greatest love was her drugs and alcohol. We decided to go to Church that Sunday, light a candle for Evie, and pray for her to rest in peace finally. Her secrets were finally out, and that was what she wanted to happen before she passed away.

Planning the wedding in the next few weeks was easy because Cathy volunteered to help with everything, and she was thrilled when I told her the news. "Well, don't you think it is strange that I am getting married at 55 years old," I asked her. "Hell no! I just rolled my eyes at her and showed her a magazine photo of a wedding dress. I think it is strange that you didn't marry the man 25 years ago," she laughed.
"What do you think of this?" I asked. It was an elegant white dress that was tea-length and form-fitting around the midsection.

It had a V-neck with lace wrapped around and slightly puffed-out short sleeves. The bottom of the dress flared out a bit, so it would twirl a bit when I danced. I absolutely adored it, and I asked Cathy if she would go with me to try it on. The next day we did just that, and I purchased the dress on the spot. I asked Cathy if I could store it at her place so that Jesse would not see it before our wedding day. She agreed. The days seemed to go by quickly; before we knew it, the wedding was a week away. I felt good about everything. I was ready for this day.

Jesse and I were married on June 19th, 2019, and a few of our closest friends from town and our family were there to celebrate our special day. The sun was shining, and the evening air was perfect. I thought of Jenni and Mike that day and felt their presence. I knew that they were both smiling down at us, and that brought me comfort. As we danced our first dance as husband and wife, Jesse leaned in and whispered to me, "I love you, Kally, and I promise you that I will make my brother proud, knowing that I will never hurt you or leave your side ever again" I laid my head on his chest, and felt safe, protected, and loved. We had finally learned how to forgive each other, forgive ourselves, and feel worthy of love again, and we embraced it wholeheartedly.

The following day, we opened our wedding gifts, and tears flooded my eyes when I opened the wedding present that Carrie had given us. She had framed the old map, circled in red Newbury, California, and Springfield, Illinois, and had engraved on a plaque, "Finally Home" I held it to my heart. I looked upward, and suddenly I felt like this old beat-up map was a gift from my daddy to help me find the home where I belonged.

He led me to Mike, and when Mike had to leave, the magic in the map continued as Mike guided me to Jesse. It comforted me to believe that Mike had to leave me so he could be there to take care of our dear Jenni, and he knew that I would need someone too, so Carrie was right; fate brought us together, and love led me home. I went over, hung the framed map on the wall, looked toward heaven, and softly whispered, "Thank you.

A WORD FROM THE AUTHOR

Thank you for taking the time to read "Fated Destination." I hope you enjoyed reading it as much as I enjoyed writing it.

My next book is in progress. Please follow to receive updates, and I would appreciate it if you could leave me a review. Thank you again.

Carla Mulcahy

Made in the USA
Middletown, DE
30 August 2023

37672751R00094